5

LP-ROM QUI
Bonfire memories
Quilford, Sally
1005272

VE DEC 2013

PL MAR 2014

VE Jun 14

SPECIAL MESSAGE TO READERS

THE ULVERSCROFT FOUNDATION
(registered UK charity number 264873)
was established in 1972 to provide funds for research, diagnosis and treatment of eye diseases. Examples of major projects funded by the Ulverscroft Foundation are:-

- The Children's Eye Unit at Moorfields Eye Hospital, London
- The Ulverscroft Children's Eye Unit at Great Ormond Street Hospital for Sick Children
- Funding research into eye diseases and treatment at the Department of Ophthalmology, University of Leicester
- The Ulverscroft Vision Research Group, Institute of Child Health
- Twin operating theatres at the Western Ophthalmic Hospital, London
- The Chair of Ophthalmology at the Royal Australian College of Ophthalmologists

You can help further the work of the Foundation by making a donation or leaving a legacy. Every contribution is gratefully received. If you would like to help support the Foundation or require further information, please contact:

THE ULVERSCROFT FOUNDATION
The Green, Bradgate Road, Anstey
Leicester LE7 7FU, England
Tel: (0116) 236 4325

website: www.foundation.ulverscroft.com

BONFIRE MEMORIES

Guy Sullivan's arrival in the quiet village of Midchester ruffles feathers and stirs up old memories, not least for Cara Baker, who had all but forgotten a frightening incident from her childhood . . . As she helps Guy find out what happened to his sister, she begins to fall in love. But she's made mistakes in the past, and with a murderer on the loose setting the village alight, Cara might get her fingers burned in more ways than one.

Books by Sally Quilford
in the Linford Romance Library:

THE SECRET OF HELENA'S BAY
BELLA'S VINEYARD
A COLLECTOR OF HEARTS
MY TRUE COMPANION
AN IMITATION OF LOVE
SUNLIT SECRETS
MISTLETOE MYSTERY
OUR DAY WILL COME

SALLY QUILFORD

BONFIRE MEMORIES

Complete and Unabridged

LINFORD
Leicester

First published in Great Britain

First Linford Edition
published 2013

Copyright © 2012 by Sally Quilford
All rights reserved

A catalogue record for this book is available from the British Library.

ISBN 978–1–4448–1759–1

Published by
F. A. Thorpe (Publishing)
Anstey, Leicestershire

Set by Words & Graphics Ltd.
Anstey, Leicestershire
Printed and bound in Great Britain by
T. J. International Ltd., Padstow, Cornwall

This book is printed on acid-free paper

1

What does Humphrey Bogart say in that film? Of all the bars in all the world . . . This isn't anything like Rick's Bar. It's The Quiet Woman pub in a miserable backwater of England. It's full of small-minded people, living small-minded lives. Their imaginations don't stretch beyond the boundaries of the village, but that suits me. It's easier to fool people like them. I smile at them, buy their drinks and they greet me like an old friend. Who would have thought loyalty came so cheap?

Then she walked in. I felt my heart somersault, just as it did the first time I saw her more than ten years ago. She's older than the last time we met but still as exquisite as ever. Motherhood has added something to her features, as if it completes her. I hate her for that. For getting more joy from the child than from me.

I realise with a start that I still love her too. She smiles at me, pleasure lighting up her beautiful blue eyes, and I shake my head quickly, hoping no-one else had noticed her.

It's a lame wish because strangers stand out here, just as I did when I first arrived. A beautiful stranger is even more noticeable. I look to the corner of the bar, where Peg Bradbourne usually sits. She's not there. Thank God!

They're all nosey around here, but old Peg has a special type of nosiness. It's more insightful. She may never have left the village, but her imagination does stretch beyond the boundaries. She would remember the beautiful visitor long after everyone else had forgotten. She would notice that the woman was looking for me. Everyone else is . . . what do they call it around here? Too much in their cups — drunk, in other words. Apart from a few who only drink lemonade, but they're a special kind of stupid, so they don't count.

I walk across the pub and whisper to the lovely newcomer in our own tongue, 'Not here.'

I see the hurt in her eyes and it crucifies me. What I really want is to hold her and kiss her and tell her how glad I am to see her. But that won't do. Not in Midchester, of all places. My reputation has been too hard won and I won't give it up now.

The woman I adore is a danger to me. I don't know what I can to do to put things right.

* * *

Midchester 1966

Guy Sullivan stood at the window of The Grange, looking down over Midchester village. He rolled his shoulders a little, feeling the walls closing in on him. It was the sort of place one either found on a chocolate box, or covered in snow on a Christmas card. The early morning frost glistening on the roof of the Norman church added something to that effect. He could see the appeal, but his reasons for being there prevented him from really enjoying the scenery.

From the moment he arrived in Midchester, he had experienced a sense of foreboding. It was a pretty little place, yet he believed there was darkness and secrets long buried amongst the back to back terraces and dim alleyways at the far end of the village. Midchester brought out his innate claustrophobia. It was something he had not suffered since he was a little boy and crammed into a dormitory with dozens of other people. The memory caused him to flex his long arms. At least he did have more room here.

He hoped he would not have to stay too long. He was used to wide-open spaces and The Grange, though one of the largest houses in the area, still seemed small compared to his sprawling mansion in Los Angeles and his sheep farm in Australia. Not that he could call either of those places home.

Guy watched as the gate at the bottom of the long driveway opened, and a red Hillman Minx came trundling up the lane. He had been given a Hillman Minx as a gift once, but had to give it away to charity when he found it impossible to drive due to his long legs.

The girl who got out was perfect for the vehicle. The epitome of the sixties, she was petite with slender legs encased in tight black slacks. She wore a black roll-neck sweater under a smock type red jacket. He couldn't see her face as the wind blew a curtain of brown hair across it just as she turned towards him.

A few moments later his personal assistant entered the drawing room and closed the door behind her. 'The young lady from the local newspaper is here, Guy.'

'Thanks, Enid. Send her in.'

'Are you sure you want to do this, Guy? You could tell them you're here on a private visit and don't wish to give interviews.'

'You know how it goes, Enid. If you don't talk to them, they keep hounding you anyway. I'll give the girl her story and then she'll be happy.'

'She might also bring the rest of the press to your door.'

'We'll see.'

'I haven't had time to brief her yet. Do you want me to tell her that some subjects are off topic?' Enid did not have to tell Guy what particular subject she referred to. The papers had been full of it for the past year. Enid was a middle-aged woman who had never had children of her own. It was one of the reasons she protected Guy so valiantly.

Guy shook his head. 'No, that never works either. Come on, let's get this over with.'

Enid nodded curtly and went back out. A few moments later, she opened the door again and announced, 'Miss Cara Baker'.

Guy put on his most winning smile and stepped forward. 'Miss Baker, thank you for coming today.'

He stopped short, stunned by a delicately pretty face and limpid blue eyes. The girl looked so fragile Guy idly wondered if she would snap if a gust of wind somehow got into the room.

'Hello, Mr Sullivan,' Cara Baker stammered. She seemed to have something stuck in her throat as she coughed between words. Guy was used to having that effect. It disappointed him to learn that she was no different to any other girl. 'You'll have to forgive me,' she said, sounding a little more composed. 'I've never interviewed a famous actor before. I've interviewed the mayor, but he's only famous in Midchester. And now I'm waffling. Sorry.'

'Yeah, but I'm not really a famous actor,' said Guy, smiling. He gestured for her to sit down on one of the plush sofas. 'Bring some tea, please, Enid.' Enid left the room again, casting a warning glance at Guy. He knew it meant to be careful. No-one could know why they were really in Midchester.

'Oh, but you are,' Cara countered. 'You're tipped for an Oscar for your latest film.'

'Yes, as best director,' said Guy, sitting on the sofa opposite her and stretching out his long legs, which were encased in blue jeans. 'My acting roles were usually to be the guy the heroine dumps so she can marry Steve McQueen or Paul Newman.'

'Does that bother you?' asked Cara. He noticed that she had not yet taken out a notebook and pencil. 'Being the guy who loses out to a better looking man? I mean, it's not that you're not good looking, you are, but . . . '

'I'm what's known as Hollywood ugly,' said Guy with a knowing smile.

'I wouldn't say you were ugly at all.'

'Thank you. You may want to write

this down,' he said, gesturing to her empty hands.

'What? Oh yes, sorry.' Cara fumbled in her bag for a notebook and pen. 'Sorry, the thing is . . . not only have I never interviewed anyone famous, you're only my second interview for the local paper. Mr Black, the editor — he's also the mayor by the way, Eric Black if you should ever meet him — he said I have to stop acting like I'm just having a chat with people and start realising I'm here to get a story. Only I can't fight the feeling that I'm just being nosy.'

'Actually a chat works for me. What would you like to chat about? Be as nosy as you like.'

'Well, you of course. Does it bother you that you have moved to directing because you didn't get the big roles?'

'Not at all. I find directing much more interesting. I get to boss people around for a start, and I really enjoy that.'

Cara laughed. 'I think I'd enjoy that

too, though my landlady, Nancy, says I already do that with everyone.' She looked down at her notepad and pressed her lips together. 'I'm waffling again. Perhaps you could start by telling me a bit about yourself. Your life story and how you became a famous actor.'

Guy paused for a moment. Should he tell her the truth or the Hollywood sanctioned story? For the sake of his new film, he decided to stick with the Hollywood version.

'I was born in Australia, thirty-six years ago. My family were descended from convicts.' Not for the first time, Guy marvelled at how, in the current climate, that was a more palatable story than the truth. 'We had our own sheep ranch. In fact, I still own that ranch.' It was only half a lie. He had bought it in nineteen-sixty. 'But I wanted to travel the world, so I went to the States and worked my way across America.' Part of what he said was true, but not all of it. 'Somehow I ended up as an extra in Hollywood. On Spartacus, no less.

Blink and you'll miss me.'

It was an old joke, but he was gratified to see that Cara smiled. Every actor had claimed to be an extra on Spartacus and there was no way of disproving it, given just how many were used for the filming. 'Then the roles got bigger. I got the odd line here and there. I played a few tough guys. Their role was to die at the hands of the hero.'

'So you've never had acting lessons?'

'I did later, when I realised acting was what I wanted to do. Believe me, my lack of acting knowledge shows in my early films. Hitchcock said I was the stiffest stiff he'd ever seen.'

It was another old joke, and in no way true, but people seemed to like it. Guy sighed. He had told so many lies, even he was not sure of the truth anymore.

'But things got better, and I got a minor role in a Paul Newman film which led to bigger roles.'

'They're saying that the war film you've just directed will solidify your place as a Hollywood bigwig.'

'You did your research really well,' said Guy.

'I erm . . . ' Cara blushed. 'I've watched a lot of your films.' She looked down at her notepad.

Guy was amused to see it was completely empty, but the story he had told could be found anywhere, and maybe she already knew it if she had done her research.

'I'm a fan,' she said in a quieter voice. 'Sorry, that was really lame of me. I'm not supposed to say things like that. I just think you're a really good actor, and I'm sure you're a brilliant director. If you don't get an Oscar, it will be a travesty.' She blushed.

'Thank you, Cara.' Guy wanted to be pleased that she liked him. She was lovely. But she might also be yet another woman who wanted his scalp for her collection.

'Could you tell me a little about the film? It hasn't come to Britain yet, but we're all dying to see it.'

'It's about love and war, prejudice and redemption.'

'The hero is German?'

At that point Enid entered with the tea tray. She looked from Guy to Cara and then back again, her eyes full of concern.

Guy pretended not to notice. 'Thank you, Enid,' he said firmly. She poured the tea and Guy could see her hands shaking, and wondered if Cara had noticed.

'Do you have a problem with a German hero, Cara?' he asked when Enid had left, slamming the door after her.

'What? Oh no. It's caused quite a stir around here though. During the war — I was only little at the time — everyone thought there was a saboteur stealing things and damaging vehicles. Except it wasn't. It was . . . Oh well, never mind. I just wondered at your choice of subject matter, giving how strongly people still feel about the war.'

'There was good and bad on both sides. Admittedly Hitler's government did more bad, but not everyone was involved in that. I wanted to tell the story of a man who wanted nothing to do with any of that, yet had no choice but to . . . '

'Follow orders?' said Cara, with a raised eyebrow.

'Keep under the radar, and not let his family get hurt,' Guy snapped. He took a deep breath. 'I guess the film explains it better than I do.'

'Sorry, yes. I shouldn't really comment until I've seen it, should I?' She smiled apologetically. 'I really do want to see it. But for now I have a list of questions that people have asked me to ask you,' she said, seemingly composing herself. She pulled a folded up sheet of paper from her handbag.

'Do you mind? Some are a bit personal, so you don't have to answer them if you don't want to.' Before Guy could answer, she started on the first question. 'Have you ever fallen in love with a leading lady?'

'No. I've been infatuated with them, but actresses are . . . ' What could he tell her? That actresses — and actors for that matter — tended to be a little self-obsessed. They left little room for anyone else to love them.

'Actresses are devoted to their careers, so they seldom feel like settling down. I'm not a Neanderthal, but I would like a wife and children one day.' It was a trite answer, but one female fans seemed to like.

'OK, another question. What sort of women do you like?'

At the moment, thought Guy, *I'm very partial to girls with light brown hair and big blue eyes*.

'I like all women,' he said, in another well-rehearsed speech. 'Blondes, brunettes, redheads. I like women of all shapes and sizes. What matters is what's in a woman's soul. Kindness and intelligence are more important.'

'You don't really believe that,' said Cara, raising an eyebrow. He could hardly believe she was challenging him! 'It's what all actors and pop-singers say, yet you never ever see them with plump girls or plain girls or just ordinary every day girls.'

'Isn't it what your female readers would like to believe?' asked Guy, laughing. There was no fooling this one.

'Yes, I suppose so.'

'Then that's what I think. And actually . . . ' he became more thoughtful. 'It isn't important what someone looks like. They can be very beautiful on the outside, but be a horrible person inside.' It was one of Guy's rare moments of telling the truth.

'Yes, you're right. Only a couple more questions. I'm sorry about this, but I've been asked to ask you about your relationship with Selina Cartier. Is it true that your affair with her broke up her marriage?'

'No, it's not true. Selina needed a friend and I was there, but I did not help or encourage her to cheat on her husband.'

'Sorry but I had to ask. One final question, Mr Sullivan.'

'Please call me Guy.'

'Guy, then. What are you doing in Midchester?'

'I'm here on a private visit.'

'Oh, it's just . . . '

'What?' Guy wondered if word had somehow managed to get out. It was impossible. Only he and Enid knew the real reason he was there. Given how much Cara already knew, it was possible that she had unearthed his true story.

'I know I've intruded on you too much today, especially as you now say you are here privately, it's just that I'm in charge of the Bonfire night celebrations, which we're holding at the village hall, and I wondered if you'd be willing to come along and judge the Guy Fawkes contest for the children. I'm sure Mr Black would do it, if we asked, but well, we really have never had anyone as famous as you here. But I don't want to intrude if you really are here privately.'

He breathed a sigh of relief. 'When is this?'

Cara looked at him as if he were mentally deficient. 'Bonfire night. The fifth of November. Guy Fawkes, the Houses of Parliament and all that.'

'Of course, forgive me. You'd think with a name like Guy, I'd know that.'

'No, sorry, I shouldn't assume you would know. I don't suppose you do it in Australia.'

'I can't say we ever did. Setting off fireworks and bonfires in November — which is the height of summer — is not a sensible thing to do in Australia.'

'So would you be interested in doing the judging?'

'Can I think about it?'

'Yes, of course.'

'You should give me your phone number and I'll call you.'

'It's in the book. The Quiet Woman pub. I work there. I live there too actually.'

'So you're a journalist, the organiser

of the Bonfire Night festivities and . . . '

'A barmaid. I'm also doing night classes in journalism.' Cara said. 'I like to keep busy.'

'I can see that. OK, Cara — may I call you, Cara? I'll call you when I've had time to think about it.'

Cara left a few minutes later. She had barely written anything on her pad, not even a few lines of shorthand. He only hoped she would represent him properly. He watched as she manoeuvred the car down the driveway. A beautiful and thoroughly modern woman. But how modern was she? In America, young people of her age were starting to ask for peace, yet Guy wondered if Cara held all the prejudices left over from the war. Would he find that in the rest of the village?

It was not that he didn't understand the prejudice, only that it made life difficult for those who had not supported the regime. Would anyone in Britain understand how hard it was for a family to survive in a dangerous era of distrust and betrayal?

This was what he had tried to portray in his first directorial debut. But Guy was smart enough to know that while Hollywood may make films about equality and the greyer areas of life, in the towns and cities the old feuds died hard. Especially those about a war that had resulted in millions of deaths and was still in living memory.

He heard the door to the drawing room open and close.

'What was all that about?' said Enid.

'The film, that's all.'

'Are you sure?'

'Absolutely. She's just a kid, Enid.'

'They're often the worst. Older people sometimes see grey areas, but for a girl like that, life is black and white.'

'Have you heard from Carl Anderson yet?' Guy turned to face his old friend.

Enid shook her head. 'No news. He said he would call today, but nothing yet.'

'I wonder what's keeping him.' Guy

ran his fingers through his hair.

'I don't know, but he said he had something important to tell us. Strange how he hasn't turned up yet.'

'Give him a call again. The sooner he tells us and we can get out of this damn place the better.'

'What's brought this on, Guy? You said it was a quaint little village when we arrived. Is this about the girl?'

'No, it's not about the girl. It's about Greta, as it's always been.' He slumped down onto the sofa. 'Why did I leave it so long to come and find her?'

'You couldn't afford the fare.'

'Ten years ago I couldn't afford the fare. I've been able to come here for years now and yet I kept putting it off.'

Enid put her hand on his shoulder. 'Why?'

'Because I'm afraid of what I'll find.' Guy put his head in his hands, fighting back the anger and pain that had lived in his heart for so long. 'But it's not about the girl. It's not.'

Or at least it should not be about the

girl. He couldn't afford to get side-tracked by a pair of pretty blue eyes. Those same eyes that would no doubt turn cold when she found out the truth about him.

2

1946

She's waiting for me when I leave the pub. I lead her along one of the darkened streets and up into the fields. There's an old Roman fort up there. It was popular with archaeologists for a while, but they soon lost interest and went in search of bigger, better digs. The night is bitter cold, yet I feel warm with the excitement of seeing her again.

'I came all this way to find you,' she says, when we reach the cover of the trees. It's so good to hear my own tongue spoken, instead of the flat vowels of the locals. The same vowels I'd had to learn by heart. Nevertheless, I look around, terrified that someone might overhear us. This soon after the war, being German in Britain is not a good idea. Especially if people found out you'd been there all along. If they saw me talking to her, they might ask questions about where I came from. My cover story would not survive too much scrutiny.

I had already managed to avoid one witch hunt, all caused by that idiot who had a grudge against the Americans at the air base. Suspicion had fallen on someone else. Not that I cared. The man was a Jew. He would not have been dealt with so kindly in the Fatherland.

'I know, my love,' I tell her, stroking her silky hair and feeling the desire rising within me. 'But you must realise how careful I have to be. If people around here realised the truth . . . '

'I would never betray you.' She says it with the simplicity of a child and I want to believe her, I really do. She always was honest. A little bit too honest. I was miserable when she went so far away, but in reality I knew she could never keep up the subterfuge needed for the work I had to do.

'I know you wouldn't, my love,' I tell

her. I hoped I sounded surer than I felt.

She reached up and stroked my cheek. 'I want to kiss you again,' she said. 'It's been so long.'

I wanted her too, desperately. I'd hidden that part of myself so deep for so long, because it was dangerous to do otherwise. Now she awakened it. I caught her hand in mine. 'Not here.'

'Not here. Not at the pub,' she said, starting to cry. She's becoming hysterical and that's even more dangerous. 'Then where? You do want to be with me, don't you? We can find a way to explain it, darling. I know we can.'

'It's not that easy. I've created a whole new identity here. You don't fit into it.'

She bites her lower lip, something she always does when she's unsure. It was one of the things that first attracted me to her. She'd had so much innocence and uncertainty in such a voluptuous body. I was glad to see she still had that, despite the baby. 'I left her to come and find you,' she says. 'I hoped we could all be together, as a family.'

'And we will, my love,' I lie. 'Just not yet. My work here isn't finished. Meet me tomorrow in Shrewsbury. There's a hotel there where we can be alone, away from the prying eyes of these people.'

She trusts me enough to nod and agree. I do want to be alone with her, just one more time. To hold her in my arms and feel her velvet flesh against mine. Then I must work out what to do with her. I must ensure that the web I've woven in Midchester does not unravel.

* * *

1966

'I'm the worst journalist in the world,' Cara groaned as she sat on her bed looking at her empty notepad.

The walls were decorated with posters of Paul McCartney and Elvis Presley. Paul stared out with innocent blue eyes and floppy brown hair. Elvis's blue eyes smouldered, beneath swept back black velvet hair. Above the bed was a smaller picture, cut from a magazine. It was of Guy Sullivan and taken from a western. He played the bad guy, and died at the end, but Cara still thought he was wonderful.

The bed was strewn with fashion magazines, most showing Twiggy and Jean Shrimpton. Cara aspired to look like either of them in turn, depending on what day of the week it was. On that day, she had gone for the Jean Shrimpton look, with straight hair, back-combed lightly to give it the devil-may-care look that had taken her over an hour to get right.

'How do you work that out?' asked Nancy. Nancy was thirty-eight years old, so more than ten years older than Cara, but they had become devoted friends. Nancy's red hair was also backcombed, much higher than Cara's, and she wore much more make up. It suited her vivacious nature.

'He was just so handsome that I completely forgot what I was supposed to be doing. Lord knows why he thinks he's Hollywood ugly, or whatever it was he said. Honestly, Nance, he's got to be at least six-foot-four, and he has the most amazing eyes. Sometimes they look blue, sometimes they look grey.' Cara rested her head on her hands. 'And his smile . . . ' She sighed. 'It's odd, because he seems sad too, but I can't work out why.'

'That'll be that Selina Cartier, the witch,' said Nancy. 'She breaks hearts wherever she goes. First that poor husband of hers and now Guy Sullivan. No wonder he had to turn to directing after that scandal. Mind you, it's different for men. Ingrid Bergman had to leave Hollywood when she got . . . well, you know.' Nancy's hands formed a bump motion on her tummy. 'Men are never judged the same.'

'There was something else,' said Cara. 'I think he was offended by what I said about his film having a German hero. I suppose it's his art. I know how upset I felt when Mr Black said the first article I tried to write for him was rubbish. It was like he was disrespecting my child. Still, he liked the next one.'

'Not enough to pay you for it,' Nancy sniffed.

'It's experience, Nance.'

'Hmm. I could say the same about you working behind the bar, but at least I pay you.'

Cara stood up and threw her arm around her friend. 'You do more than that. You're the best. I'm finally starting to feel as if I'm being accepted by folks. I'm no longer seen as one of the dreadful Baker family. Honestly,' she said, going to the wardrobe to find a nice dress for the lunchtime shift, 'you'd think with one of my brothers going to Oxford University, another one in the air force, and our Millie working for the government, people would forget that we were once the poorest family in Midchester.'

Cara's mother, Martha Baker, had moved to the village with her four older children just before the war, when Cara's father was called up. Until then they had been travellers, moving from place to place. Mrs Baker, widowed soon after her husband went abroad, and heavily pregnant with Cara, had found it difficult to settle into village life. The gossip of the local women, who worried far too much than was good for them about the hue of Mrs Baker's white sheets and the fact that the children wore frayed hand-me-downs, did not help.

Things had been a little better since Mrs Baker remarried and became Mrs Potter, but Cara still often felt the weight of the villagers' disapproval. Cara's own recent transgression had not helped. She sensed that they had been waiting for her to fail just so they could say that they had seen it coming a mile off.

'Don't you know it's poor people's fault that they're poor?' Nancy quipped.

'Seriously, pet, people can't forgive poverty, because they're terrified it will be them one day.'

'Yet old Peg Bradbourne isn't rich, and everyone treats her like the queen. Not that she doesn't deserve it. She's lovely.' Peg had been one of the few people to show kindness to the struggling Martha Baker.

'Ah, but that's genteel poverty. It's quite a different thing. How old is that woman now? Eighty-five? Ninety? Yet she'll be there at lunchtime, in the same seat at the bar, waiting for her bottle of stout. She's going to see us all off.'

Nancy stopped at the posters of McCartney and Presley, looking at them appreciatively. 'You know, I think Paul is the type of man you marry. But Elvis . . . Mmm, I'd have other less respectable plans for him and his swivelly hips . . . ' She winked at Cara, and left the room.

True to Nancy's word, Peg Bradbourne was the first one through the door when they opened the pub.

The Quiet Woman pub was in the centre of Midchester, and as such the hub of all the gossip and information. It had been owned by Nancy's uncle, Tom Yeardley. He sold it to Nancy when he and his second wife decided to move to America. His only child, a daughter, had married an American airman, and Tom wanted to be able to spend his final years with his grandchildren.

There had been a lot of gossip about a woman running a pub, but Nancy was mostly impervious to such criticism. She soon proved she could be just as tough as her Uncle Tom when she needed to be. Only when the bar closed did she moan to Cara about the way she was treated, particularly by the men. There had been uproar when she installed a juke box in the pub and it gathered dust in the corner. The only time music played on it was after closing time when Nancy and Cara liked to listen to The Beatles' *Twist and Shout* as they cleared everything away.

'What can I get you, Peg?' said Cara,

smiling at their first guest. 'A Harvey Wallbanger? A martini, shaken not stirred? A champagne cocktail?'

Peg's old eyes twinkled. 'That's what you get for hobnobbing with the rich and shameless, is it?' She jumped up onto her stool with the energy of a five year old. 'I saw you, driving up The Grange this morning.'

'Not much gets past you, Peg.'

Cara put a bottle of stout and a glass on the counter. Peg's nosiness was different to everyone else's. There was no malice to it. She just liked to know what was going on, and considered herself something of a sleuth.

'So?' said Peg. 'What's he like?'

'Oh he's very handsome,' said Cara. 'But sad too.' It did not occur to her to keep anything from the village's First Lady.

'Sad? Why?'

'He's here on private business, so I didn't like to pry.'

'Call yourself a reporter?' Peg grinned cheekily.

'Oh, I know, I'm awful . . . '

'Now,' said Peg, reaching across the bar and patting Cara's hand, 'I don't mean to be unkind, pet. You're the hardest working girl in Midchester. It's not a bad thing that you're fazed by a nice looking man. It shows you're human. I must go up and meet this Mr Sullivan.'

'Oh be careful, Peg. There's this woman, Enid, who is his secretary or something. She's very fierce and protective of him. You can tell.'

'In love with him, do you think?'

'Oh I don't think so. She's old enough to be his mum.'

'Tsk,' Peg pursed her lips, and winked. 'Just because a woman reaches a certain age doesn't mean she's not partial to a nice bit of cream cake.'

Cara laughed. 'My life would probably be much simpler if I stuck to cream cake and left men alone.'

'Oh well,' said Peg, 'everyone is entitled to one mistake, pet, and you didn't know, did you?'

'Yeah, but it was a pretty big mistake as far as the village is concerned.' Cara did not want to think of the past, so she shook her head to clear away the thoughts. 'But that is in the past. I won't be that stupid again.'

More people came into the bar, so Cara went to help Nancy serve them. It was the usual lunchtime crowd. Mr and Mrs Simpson, who had recently moved into a new bungalow opposite the pub, Herbie Potter, the postman, who was Cara's stepfather, and a few other villagers. Mr Simpson and Herbie went into the bar with the men, while Mrs Simpson joined the other ladies in the lounge. Nancy had once tried to introduce a mixed bar, but even her resolve could not make it work. The men and women liked their separate spheres in the pub.

Cara knew that Peg liked to sit at the bar in the lounge because she could see both rooms from her stool. Peg also had very good hearing, so did not miss any conversation.

'So I looked at the broken roof tile,' said Mrs Simpson, 'and I said, 'Mon dieu, how did that happen?' Then they sorted it out, voila!' Since her son had married a French girl during in the war, she peppered most of her speech with Gallic phrases, much to the amusement of everyone else in the village.

'So when are you going to visit that son of yours in France, Myrtle?' asked Peg.

'Len won't go. It's not that we don't love Monique and the children, but well . . . Len says they're very French over there.'

'Really?' Peg had a twinkle in her eye. She winked at Cara, who was serving the ladies. 'Who'd have thought that?'

Cara stifled a giggle and got on with her work. She could only pick up bits of gossip as she served customers and cleared tables. Mr Black, the mayor and newspaper owner, was having a dinner party, and some of the younger women in the village were going to help serve, while a couple of the men were going to look after the guest's vehicles. Herbie Potter was saying there might be a strike at the Post Office over pay and hours, but he got little sympathy as everyone considered him to have the easiest job in the area.

'You stop by home every morning for a bacon sandwich,' said Len Simpson. 'I didn't have much chance of that when I was working down the pit.'

There was some talk about the situation in Rhodesia, but that seemed so far away and had so little to do with the insular world of Midchester, no-one had much to say other than that it was a 'rum job'.

Mainly people were talking about the impending Bonfire Night celebrations. That was real and immediate. With Midchester being such a quiet village and with only one pub, any sort of event was treated like a jubilee celebration.

'Do you remember,' Len Simpson was saying, 'when someone was convinced they found that body in the bonfire?'

Cara stopped what she was doing to listen. She had a vague recollection of hearing the story before, but could not remember when. 'When was this, Mr Simpson?'

'Oh, now let me see. It must have been after the war, because we couldn't have bonfires and firework displays during the blackout, and before the war we didn't really do much of that sort of thing. It was old Tom Yeardley who started it all up again. It got us all in a lather, it did. But when we went out there to look and it was nothing. Just an old Guy Fawkes effigy.'

'It was Cara who found it,' said Herbie Potter, quietly. 'Don't you remember, lass?'

'No.' Did she? Cara felt an icy tingle on her spine. She tried to recall the scene, but to no avail. That did not stop her feeling suddenly cold and afraid.

'Well, you were only about five or six at the time.' Herbie said, turning to the pub landlady, 'Nancy, you must remember it, because we all thought young Sammy Granger was behind it, the little — ' Herbie paused, remembering that the ladies, though in the next room, might hear him, ' — the little tyke disappeared a day or two after, and he's never been seen since.'

'I remember now,' said Len Simpson, nodding. 'We thought it was him, because a couple of days earlier him and his friends had pulled this stunt where one of them dressed up in ragged clothes and stuck newspaper out of the armholes, reckoning to be an effigy at the Guy Fawkes contest. It made us all laugh, but no-one was fooled. Sammy was a rum 'un though. Good riddance to bad rubbish, I say.'

'Sammy was alright,' said Nancy, hotly. 'He couldn't help that his mother drank too much and didn't care where he was. He was clever and given half a chance . . . '

The telephone in the back hallway began to ring, stopping Nancy from completing her statement.

'Oh, still holding that candle, hey?' said Len, to general laughter around the room.

Nancy slammed a pint of beer on the bar and went to answer the telephone. When she returned she looked pale. Cara, who had taken glasses back to the bar, ready to wash them, heard her say 'Of all the things . . . '

'What is it, Nancy?'

'What?' It seemed as if Nancy had just been woken from a dream. 'Nothing, just that the delivery might be a bit late tomorrow. Cara, I have to nip out as soon as we close. Can you finish up here?'

'Well, OK, but I do have to . . . ' Cara smiled wryly. 'I have to go and talk to Mrs Cunningham about the rules for the Guy Fawkes effigy contest, would you believe? I'm meeting her in the Village Hall. I think they call that synchronicity. Or coincidence or something.'

'There's a lot of that about,' said Nancy, pressing her lips together firmly.

Cara went over to Peg and, without needing to be told, changed the empty bottle of stout for a full one. Lowering her voice, because she didn't want to face teasing from the customers again, she said, 'Do you remember me finding that body, Peg?'

'Oh yes, dear. You were really shaken up about it, if I remember rightly. You insisted that the effigy must have got up and walked away. It took your mum ages to calm you down.'

Cara felt a bit queasy, because the memory was there, somewhere, but she just could not dredge it up. When she tried, the image was unreal, like that of a picture book. 'How have I managed to forget it?'

'Oh, because it turned out to be nothing, I suppose. Had it been a real body, it would have stuck in your mind better.'

'And you're sure it wasn't?'

'Yes. Whatever makes you ask that, dear?'

'I don't know. It must have been a

very good effigy to make me think it moved.'

'You were a child, with an imagination as big as the Pacific Ocean, Cara. Children think monsters live under their beds and can swear blind they hear them. They have no trouble conjuring up a Guy Fawkes that moves.'

'But . . . ' The images in Cara's head were becoming clearer, but she did not know if she could trust them.

'What?'

Cara shook her head. 'Oh, nothing. I'm probably dredging up more fantasies now because I can't really remember.' She put glasses into the sink under the counter.

'Well if you ever want to talk about it . . . ' She could feel Peg's shrewd eyes watching her as she washed the glasses. 'I do like a mystery, even one that's been solved.'

'Thanks, Peg.'

She should ask Herbie more about it, or her mother. Why she needed to know she did not understand. After all, it was something that had happened years ago. She had made a stupid mistake as a child that inconvenienced everyone and then amused them. She could just hear the villagers muttering 'stupid kid', after they had come out of their warm homes.

It shouldn't matter in the big scheme of things, but for Cara, who had spent most of her childhood having fingers pointed at her because of her traveller heritage, it felt like another mark of shame. 'You're an idiot,' she told herself, laughing at her own hyperbole as she washed the glasses.

Yet she'd always disliked Bonfire Night, preferring to stay in and read a book while the family went to the organised displays. It made her place as organiser this year ironic. For Cara, getting involved was a way of feeling like one of the villagers and not the outsider she had always considered herself to be.

By the end of the lunchtime session,

and after Cara had cleaned up, dusk was beginning to fall. She put on a thick coat and made her way towards the Village Hall. It was a foggy evening again and she hoped that the heavy pall over the village would lift in time for Bonfire Night, otherwise the fireworks they had bought would be a waste of time.

As she walked along the main street of Midchester and turned a corner towards the village hall, which was next door to the Church, she could only see a few feet ahead. Keeping in close to the buildings, so she could avoid walking into the road, she passed by comforting domestic scenes. Blazing fires lit up sitting rooms and children sat in front of the telly, watching The Wooden Tops.

She began to wish she was inside rather than out on such a grim evening. At one point, she was sure that she heard footsteps behind her. Or were they ahead of her? It was hard to tell. As she walked, she tried to remember the incident from when she was a child. But the more she tried to bring it to the forefront of her mind, the more it remained in shadow.

Instead it led to other memories, such as her mother's remarriage to Herbie Potter and each of her siblings going off into the world, while she stayed behind in Midchester. So she tried to recall that night again, but that only led to other memories of being bullied at school and the villagers who looked down on her and her family. Those memories led to her feeling tense, and it was almost as if all those accusing people were hiding in the fog waiting for her. She could even hear their footsteps as they verbally abused her and then ran away. Then she became sure they were real footprints that she heard.

'Who is it?' She longed for a voice to answer and alleviate her fears but no-one replied, which only increased her fears. She tried to calm down. After all, she had walked the streets of

Midchester all her life and at all times of the day. Yet for the first time she sensed malevolence in the air. For no good reason, she believed it was aimed at her. No, it was not the first time. She had felt that malevolence before, a long time ago.

Concentrating on not bumping into anything, and trying to hold back the tide of fear, she almost fell over the legs that were sticking out on the ground. A cold hand clutched her heart, and she very nearly screamed.

Oh yes, Cara, she thought, as she struggled to compose herself. *Make a fuss over some effigy again and you won't get away with it this time*.

She stooped down to push the Guy Fawkes out of the way, so that no-one else would fall over it. But her hands did not touch old cloth, stuffed with newspaper. They touched a very solid set of warm legs.

'Hello?' Cara said, — tentatively, thinking maybe one of the older villagers had tripped over in the fog.

'Who is this?' She moved her hands to the person's head, but when she touched it, it flopped over. Cara gasped, trying to assess the situation.

In the blink of an eye, the past came to her as clearly as if it were happening in front of her eyes. She had spent all that day, twenty years ago, reading a Ladybird book about Guy Fawkes and the Gunpowder Plot. The image of him and his effigy had stuck in her mind. Her mother had sent her to the corner shop to get some sugar, with the promise of bonfire toffee after tea. It was only a few doors away from their home, but Cara's head was full to the brim with gunpowder, treason and plot. Enthralled by the big pile of wood she could see in the distance, she wandered off towards the village green where the first Bonfire Night party after the war was to be held.

She had seen fireworks when the war ended and had longed to see more. Soon that would happen again and the big pile of wood in front of her would light up the night sky. She saw the effigy resting against the side of the bonfire and, in her childish way, assumed it had fallen from the top. She moved in closer. Her brothers had been making a Guy Fawkes, but this one was better. It looked real. Amused and excited, Cara had reached out and touched it. Like the figure in the fog some twenty years later, the head fell forward, and that was when little Cara realised she was not looking at a model. It was a real person and they were hurt. The malevolence that haunted her for weeks afterwards filled the night air. She did not see anyone else, but she sensed there was someone lurking nearby.

She cried out and ran back to her mother, forgetting the sugar. On seeing her stricken daughter, Martha had roused Herbie from his place by the fire. He in his turn had called upon Len, who got all the other men out looking.

When they returned it was with much teasing of Cara. There was no

Guy Fawkes on the Bonfire. Cara had been furious with them for laughing at her, and had gone to bed that night crying, 'There was, there was.'

And there had been. Twenty years later, Cara was convinced she had not imagined it. The figure leaning against the bonfire had felt as real as the person lying on the ground on a cold November evening in nineteen-sixty-five.

Less than a second had passed as all the memories flooded her mind. He needed help, of that she was certain; her hands were wet and sticky, and even though it was difficult to make out the substance in the dim light, she knew it was blood. A wave of nausea rose in the back of her throat.

A hand touched her shoulder and a vaguely familiar voice said her name. That was when Cara really screamed.

3

1946

We meet at the hotel in Shrewsbury. It's a discreet place I've used before. They don't much care how you sign the register. So Mr and Mrs Smith it is.

Despite all the times we've made love in the past, we're shy with each other tonight. Between us is something unspoken and, to me, unspeakable.

'It's been so long,' she whispers, curving her body into mine. 'I've forgotten how good you feel.'

I tell her the same, and I mean it, despite thoughts of her betrayal racing through my head. As I hold her to me, I remember the pleasure we found in each other before the war. Is it so wrong of me to take that pleasure again?

Being close to her reminds me of the

pain of that parting. It was the second time she had betrayed me. The first time resulted in a child that could never be mine, no matter how much she wanted us to live as a family. The second time was when she got on a boat to Australia, leaving not just me, but the Fatherland behind.

The worst of it is that I told her to go. Deep down I hoped she would choose me. Instead she chose the child and six years in an internment camp. She wrote to me soon afterwards, begging forgiveness, but I ignored her letters.

Still I hold her to me in this shabby hotel room. I might as well make the most of the time we have.

'I'll never love anyone as I love you,' I tell her, truthfully.

'Then nothing else matters. We can be together.'

She thinks this is the beginning whereas I know it's the end.

* * *

'I'm so sorry, Cara,' said Guy, helping her to her feet. 'I didn't mean to make you jump, but I'd said your name a couple of times and you didn't answer.'

'I didn't hear you,' Cara said, her mind still lost somewhere in the past. 'I think this man is hurt.' She didn't have time to wonder why Guy Sullivan was there.

Guy kneeled down and lifted the man's head toward the street lamp. 'Oh my God,' he said. 'It's Carl Anderson. I had an appointment with him this afternoon but he didn't turn up. I came down the village to see if I could find him.' He tested Anderson's pulse and shook his head, grimly. 'He's dead.'

Cara's heart leapt, even though it was as she suspected. 'He's covered in blood. Do you think he fell and hurt himself?' Even as Cara asked the question, she knew that was not the case. His death had the same synchronicity as her getting ready to judge the

Guy Fawkes contest, just as she was reminded of finding a body on the bonfire some twenty years before.

'I'd be surprised if he had,' Guy said in grim tones. 'We'd better call an ambulance and the police.'

'There's a phone in the village hall,' said Cara.

'I'll stay here. That is if you don't mind going up there alone.'

Cara tried a reassuring smile and failed. 'I'll be ok, I'm sure. I'll be back in a few minutes.'

Afraid she might trip in the fog, she walked as fast as she could towards the village hall, relieved to see there was a light on. It meant that Meredith Cunningham was already there.

Halfway there she turned back. In the shifting fog, and under the street light, she could just about make out Guy stooping over Carl Anderson. For a moment she felt certain he was looking through Anderson's pockets, but the fog shifted and she put it down to a trick of the light. After all, why would he do such a thing? To help eradicate the suspicion, Cara started running, mindless of the fog and eager to get some sort of help.

'Mrs Cunningham . . . ' she said, breathlessly, as she almost fell through the door, 'there's been an accident . . . someone is dead . . . we need . . . '

'I'll get on the phone to the police,' said Meredith Cunningham. 'Sit down, Cara. As soon as I've finished I'll make you a cup of tea.'

Meredith Cunningham was a vibrant woman in her thirties, with strawberry blonde hair. People were often surprised to learn that she was married to the local vicar, Andrew Cunningham. But he was not the average vicar either, and had arrived in Midchester in the fifties, carrying a bunch of rock 'n' roll records, immediately winning the hearts of the female parishioners. The only woman who won his heart was Meredith and they had been together ever since.

Meredith was also Peg Bradbourne's

niece, and the likeness was obvious to anyone who had met them both. One day Meredith would have the same owl-like eyes as her aunt, and was already every bit as insightful. At that moment in time she was a stunning splash of colour in a sometimes drab village.

'I have to go back. Guy — Mr Sullivan — is with him.'

'If the man is already dead there's little you can do,' said Meredith as she headed for the small office which held the telephone. 'And you might disturb some important evidence.'

Meredith had picked up her aunt's taste for sleuthing. In fact, from what Cara knew of village history, it was something that everyone got involved in at some time or another. She often wondered if it was a symptom of the village's insularity. They seemed to prefer solving their own mysteries and didn't always take kindly to outsiders coming in, even if they were the police.

Cara knew that what Meredith said

about staying put made sense, but some instinct told her she had to go back as soon as possible. It was almost as if she was afraid that when she got there both the dead man and Guy Sullivan would be gone, just like the effigy had been gone twenty years before. Accepting that was the reason she wanted to return, she muttered something to Meredith, who was already on the phone, and left the hall.

When she got there, she saw that a few people had come out of their houses, including the Simpsons and her mother and step-father. News must have travelled fast, as the Simpsons and the Potters lived in different parts of the village, and neither part was particularly close to where the man's body was lying.

Anderson lay on the ground, exactly where she had left him. That was something at least.

'What's gone on here?' she heard Len Simpson ask Guy.

'This man is dead,' said Guy, with a

calmness that Cara envied. Her own heart was hammering in her chest.

'And exactly how did he get that way?'

'I found him,' Cara chipped in, pushing through the small crowd that had gathered. 'I was on my way to the village hall and fell over him. Mr Sullivan arrived afterwards.'

Her voice faded away so that it sounded unconvincing even to herself. Had Guy arrived afterwards? She only assumed he had, but the image of Guy rifling through Anderson's clothes would not leave her. Perhaps he'd been there all along, and she had just disturbed him while he was attacking Anderson. What might the dead man have that Guy Sullivan wanted?

'What she says is correct,' said Guy. 'I had an appointment with Mr Anderson up at the Grange, but he failed to turn up. I'd come down to the village to see if I could find him.'

That he told everyone exactly the same story he had told Cara made her feel more secure. No doubt he would have proof of the appointment, and if he had really wanted to kill Anderson, he could have done so in private at the Grange and no-one would have known about it. She had little doubt that the fiercely devoted Enid would help him bury the body in the back garden.

'Who is he then?' asked Herbie Potter.

As Herbie spoke, Cara's mother broke away from him and came to Cara, putting her arm around her shoulders. 'Are you alright, sweetheart?' she whispered.

'Yes, Mum, but it's exactly the same as before.' Cara wanted to listen to what Guy said but didn't want to ignore her mother.

'What do you mean?'

'Like when I saw the body on the bonfire. I know it was a real person,' Cara whispered urgently.

Martha Potter pressed her lips together in a thin line. 'I thought you'd forgotten about that.'

'Mr Simpson and Herbie reminded me today in the pub.'

'Then I want a word with you, Herbie Potter,' Martha said, her voice rising.

'What?' Herbie frowned.

'Do you know how long it took for this child to stop having nightmares after she thought she saw that body? Of course you do, because you were there. I told you it wasn't to be mentioned anymore, didn't I?'

'She's a grown up now, love. I didn't think it would matter.'

'You all doubted her, but I never did,' said Mrs Potter.

'What body is this?' Guy Sullivan's deep voice cut into the conversation.

'It happened when I was a little girl,' Cara explained. 'I'd forgotten until today. It was exactly this time of year and we had a fireworks party planned. But I thought . . . I know I found a body on the bonfire.'

'But there was nothing there when we all went to look,' said Len Simpson.

'So we figured it was just a child's overactive imagination.' His tone said that he still believed that.

'There was plenty time for someone to shift it,' said Mrs Potter. 'Herbie didn't go out for ten minutes after Cara come in crying about it. Then none of you believed it either. But I knew my girl didn't lie.'

'Martha, no-one said she was lying,' said Mrs Simpson.

'It was implied. You've accused my kids of all sorts over the years, because we used to be travellers. You more than anyone Myrtle Simpson.'

'Well I . . . If we're going to start flinging accusations, I might remind you that Herbie here is no angel.'

'Herbie knew that what he did was wrong, and he's been a good father to my children ever since.'

'Does any of this really matter?' Once again, Guy Sullivan stopped the conversation. He was a natural leader, and his commanding tones halted everyone in their tracks.

'It mattered to me,' Cara said, quietly. 'It isn't nice to be labelled a liar. And I'm sure it mattered to the dead person I found as well.'

'Yes, of course it did, Cara,' he said in a kinder voice. 'I meant the neighbourly feuds and who did what to whom and when. People are arguing and a dead man lies at their feet.'

'Sorry,' said Mrs Potter.

'Sorry,' said everyone else in turn.

Cara was put in mind of a classroom full of children having been chastised by the teacher. She felt that way herself, looking down at her feet. What must Guy Sullivan think of them all bickering over the body of a dead man?

The police and ambulance arrived, and at the same time Meredith Cunningham came from the village hall to say she had made everyone tea. There weren't many takers and Cara guessed the women would be missing Ena Sharples on Coronation Street tonight because they had a real life drama.

Cara, who did not want to stand looking at the body anymore, walked back up to the hall. The policeman in charge said he would meet her up there later to take her statement.

When she reached the hall, Meredith handed her a cup of tea and led her to a chair. It was at a long teak table, along with several other chairs. The plans for the Bonfire Night celebrations were in a buff folder at the end, reminding Cara of how her day should have panned out. 'I think we should get the doctor to come and look at you,' she said.

'Why? I'm not ill,' said Cara.

'No, love, but you've had a fright.'

'Have you ever seen a dead body?'

Meredith nodded. 'In Midchester one can hardly move without falling over them.' She pressed her lips together. 'I'm sorry, that was really crass of me.'

'But probably true,' said Cara with a wan smile.

'Sadly true. I used to think Aunt Peg exaggerated, but Midchester has seen far too much crime for such a small place.' Meredith looked over her shoulder as the door to the hall opened and a few stragglers arrived. 'I think it's all those suppressed emotions. No-one dares show their true feelings, and when they finally do, they go a bit overboard.' She patted Cara on the shoulder. 'I'll go and boil another kettle. Have a custard cream. The sugar will do you good.'

'I wish doctors gave out the same advice as you,' said Cara, picking up a biscuit, but she found that she could not eat it. Her stomach was too churned up.

'It must have been very frightening for you.' It took her a moment to realise that Guy was standing at the other side of the table and addressing her. He sat down and picked up a biscuit, nibbling at the end, but it seemed he was not that hungry either.

'I didn't even remember till today,' she said. 'Now I do remember, I wish that I didn't.'

'I know it's difficult, but can you remember what the figure looked like?'

Cara shook her head, wondering why it mattered to him. 'No, not really. Whenever I try to remember I see it as a picture. I'd been reading about the Gunpowder Plot you see, and it appeared to me almost like a drawing in a Ladybird book.'

'That was probably your childish way of dealing with it.'

'I'm not a child anymore.'

'No, but such memories hold solid. Especially if they're repressed. When I think back to the war I see it all in black and white, even my own life strangely enough, because that's how we saw it all at the cinema. I'm sure we did have colours then, but I can't remember them.'

'Is that why your film is in black and white? Hardly any films are nowadays. Not from Hollywood anyway.'

'That's very astute of you. Yes, that is why. I thought it added to the grittiness of the drama. Some might say that's pretentious but . . . ' Guy hesitated. 'This seems the wrong thing to be discussing at this moment in time.'

'Yes, of course. I'm sorry.'

'No, don't be. I'd like to talk to you about it some other time. I'd be interested to know what you think when you've seen it.'

Cara wondered why it mattered to him what she thought of his film. 'I wish I'd thought to ask you all these things earlier, instead of the stupid questions about your favourite colour and what sort of women you like.'

Guy laughed softly. 'Would the readers of the local newspaper care about my artistic vision?'

'No, probably not.' She grimaced. 'Actually they might, but you'd have to buy them a few drinks first.'

'Then you asked the right questions, Cara. In my experience no-one ever wants to know about the stuff that's really important to the actor or director.'

At that moment it seemed important

for Cara to ask the right questions. 'Did you know Mr Anderson well?'

'Not really,' said Guy. 'He was doing some work for me.'

'To do with films?' Cara asked eagerly.

'No.' He sighed, and seemed reluctant to say anything else. 'It was some other business.' His eyes took on a haunted look.

She knew she should ask him more questions. After all, she was training to be a journalist. Unfortunately, she had not quite got over the idea that she was prying into people's private lives. It was something she would have to learn to do if she was ever going to be good enough to give up working in the pub and write for a proper newspaper. At that moment in time, with Carl Anderson lying dead in the street surrounded by a police cordon, such prying seemed inappropriate.

Cara was beginning to wonder if she had chosen the wrong career path. In the pub people gave up information without anyone asking. Sometimes there was too much information. People had a tendency to tell her more than she ever wanted to know. It seemed wrong to go into people's homes and ask them searching questions with a view to telling the entire readership of a newspaper.

The police arrived and took over the tiny office, calling people one by one to question them about what they had seen. As the first on the scene, Cara told them all that she knew. She was about to tell them about Guy seeming to check Anderson's pockets, but something stopped her. After all, she didn't know if that was really the case. It had been foggy and the night was drawing in. It would be wrong to get him into trouble if she was mistaken. At least that's what she told herself. She felt sure she would not protect him if she thought he had done wrong.

Guy went in after her. She wished she could hear what he was saying to the police. He was in there a long time, which caused some muttering amongst those sitting in the hall.

Cara's mum arrived, and sat next to her, putting her arm around her. 'Are you alright, sweetheart?' Martha Potter asked for the second time that night.

'Yes, Mum, I'm fine. I told you.'

'Why don't you come home for tea? There's always plenty.'

'I have to get back to the pub soon, Mum.' Cara had tried phoning Nancy to explain her lateness, but there had been no answer. She hoped Nancy wasn't expecting her to open up. Not that it mattered. Anyone who might be in the pub was in the village hall, even if they didn't need to be there. Something exciting had happened in Midchester and nobody wanted to miss that.

When Guy eventually came out of the office, Cara thought he might come and say goodbye to her. Instead he just left the hall, seemingly in a rush, his features dark and anguished. The policeman who had questioned him stood at the office door, grimly watching Guy leave.

'Mum, I have to go,' said Cara. Without waiting for her mum to reply, she left the hall, and ran down the path, hoping to catch up with him.

'Guy,' she called, when she saw a tall, shadowy figure ahead in the street. 'Mr Sullivan, I need to ask you something.'

She turned around and made sure no-one else was there. The man in front of her stopped, and appeared to wait. She felt that same malevolence again. The one that haunted her as a child and which had filled the air just before she fell over Carl Anderson's body.

Was that Guy all along? Yet she had not felt that when he was talking to her in the hall. Then again, he was an actor and able to switch his emotions on and off at will.

'I need to ask you,' Cara said, determined not to be intimidated, 'why did you go through Mr Anderson's pockets?'

The man, whoever he was, coughed softly, almost as if he was covering up some emotional outburst, then he walked on, disappearing into the fog.

4

1946

'Tell me what you've been doing,' she asks. She's bathed and in a bathrobe. Her damp blonde hair curling around her face.

'You know that I cannot.'

'Why are you still here? The war is over. The Fuhrer is dead.'

'And he will live again. At least his cause will. I stay to be ready for that day.'

'It's over,' she tells me. 'It will be a long time before they allow Germany to have complete autonomy again.'

'Have you been reading books again?' I raise an eyebrow, and am gratified to see that the insult has hit home.

'I may not have my father's intellect, or even yours, but I'm not stupid.' She gets up and flounces to the bathroom. When she comes out, she is dressed again. 'I'd forgotten how cruel you can be,' she whispers, grabbing her bag.

I get up off the bed and take her by the hand, knowing that I cannot let her go. She knows too much about me, and now I've made her angry. Who knows what she might do in retaliation?

As if she's read my mind she says, 'I would never betray you, no matter how you might hurt me.'

'I know, my love.' I smile and hold out my arms to her. 'Come and see me again.' I tell her the address and when to come. 'Make sure you don't see or speak to anyone. At least until we can sort this out.'

Because she is honest, she believes everyone else to be. She is as trusting as a child, and I know she will do whatever I tell her to do. She always did in the past.

* * *

1966

As Cara feared, there was no-one at the pub when she got back. Not even Peg

Bradbourne. She tidied herself up a little, and set things out, putting chairs on the floor and beer mats on the tables, before unlocking the doors.

She needn't have worried. It was a while before anyone came. In fact, Nancy arrived with the first of the drinkers.

'I'm so sorry, pet,' she said to Cara. 'I got waylaid.' She looked around her and frowned. 'This lot are late tonight.'

'Nancy,' said Cara, 'don't you know what's happened?'

'What, love? What's happened?'

'I found a man dead in the street near the village hall.'

Nancy visibly paled. 'Who was it?'

'A man called Carl Anderson. He's not local but it was awful.'

'What is it?' Nancy lifted the hatch to the bar and joined Cara behind it. Cara wasn't sure but thought Nancy looked relieved.

'I'll tell you in a while. We ought to serve the customers first.'

Cara said that because the customers

were all listening with avid attention to the two women talking, she did not feel comfortable speaking in front of them. There was enough gossip in Midchester.

Half an hour later when everyone, including Peg Bradbourne, was sitting in their usual seats with their usual drinks, Cara took Nancy into the back passageway and filled her in on everything that had happened.

'I think I might even have spoken to his killer, Nancy. Only I didn't realise it at the time. I thought it was Mr Sullivan — Guy. It might have been. Oh I don't know. I'm so confused. He seems really nice, but he has a secret, I know he does.'

'Well you're the journalist, pet, you ask him.'

'I can't. In fact I'm giving up journalism. I'm not cut out for it.'

'Rubbish. You're a lovely writer. I've seen your stories and poems. You had them published as well, so they must be good.'

Cara smiled. Her publishing history included having stories and poems published in magazines that don't exactly pay for content. In one case, she'd made the mistake of paying a publisher to include one of her poems in their anthology. It was a lesson hard learned.

'Yes, but they're not real, are they? They're fiction. They don't involve me delving into other people's secrets.'

'Oh I don't know,' said Nancy with a mischievous grin. 'I thought I recognised a few Midchester folk in them.'

'Well, perhaps . . . ' Cara smiled back. 'But anyway, this is serious, Nancy. I don't have what it takes to solve this mystery. It would help if I didn't like him quite so much. What if he's a killer? I've already made one mistake with a man. I don't think I could bear to be wrong again. Not that Mr Sullivan is remotely interested in me.'

There was a low coughing sound from the bar. It was someone trying to get attention. 'Sorry,' called Nancy. 'We'll be right there.'

'That's alright,' said Peg Bradbourne, her old eyes bright and alert, as Nancy and Cara went back to the bar. 'But you have a new customer, Cara.'

Guy Sullivan was standing at the bar. He was so tall that he had to stoop a little so he could see her under the glasses which hung from above the bar. In fact, he was so tall, that he probably had to bend down to get past the thick wooden beams that crossed the ceiling.

'Hello, Cara.'

Cara was so flummoxed by him being there that she forgot her manners. 'Oh I'm so sorry, Mr Sullivan. What can I get you?'

'I'll have a pint of bitter, please. Is there anywhere we can talk privately?'

That drew a lot of looks from the customers, who had fallen into silence at the appearance of a newcomer to the pub.

'Take him to the snug,' said Nancy.

The snug was to one side of the bar.

It had access to the bar, but the rest of it was closed off to the other customers. It wasn't entirely sound-proof, but it did muffle conversation.

'I have to work,' said Cara.

'I'm sure I can manage,' said Nancy, brightly. 'We don't get many coach parties around here, at least not in November. Go on, I'll bring your drinks over.'

'Just bring me a stout before you go, please Cara,' said Peg.

Cara did so while Nancy showed Guy to the snug.

'It seems to me he's very interested in you,' Peg muttered under her breath.

'Peg Bradbourne,' said Cara, trying not to laugh. 'You really are incorrigible. You heard everything, didn't you?'

'There's a reason I like this seat,' said Peg, winking.

It was hard to be angry with Peg about her eavesdropping, but Cara couldn't help blushing to know that Peg had heard her admit to liking Guy. 'Peg . . . '

'My lips are sealed. Now go on, don't keep the young man waiting. And when you've done you can tell me all about this Carl Anderson chap. I've heard all sorts from this lot. Some say he was an undercover policeman. Others that he was here to shut down the mine. None of it is helpful.'

'I don't know who he was, Peg.'

'No, but you can give me an unbiased version of the story.'

As Cara went to join Guy in the snug, she pondered that she was not so sure about that. It was hard to be unbiased where Guy Sullivan was concerned.

'Sorry to keep you waiting,' she said as she sat down. Nancy had poured her a ladies' glass of lager and lime but she wasn't sure she wanted it. She took a sip anyway, to help lubricate her dry mouth. 'What did you want to talk to me about?'

Guy looked around him. The pub was too quiet. Everyone was trying to listen to their conversation.

'Alright you lot,' said Peg from her side of the bar. 'Get on with your conversations and stop listening to the young couple.'

Cara blushed profusely but Peg's words had the desired effect and people seemed to decide that Cara and Guy were just a couple of young lovers wanting an intimate chat, rather than two people who had insight into the murder. The pub filled with the normal level of chatter.

'I like her,' said Guy.

'Yes, Peg's great. A bit nosey, but in a nice way.'

'You'll have to introduce me later.'

'What did you want to talk about? Was it the question I asked you earlier?'

'What question?'

'It was you, when I came out of the village hall, wasn't it?'

Guy shook his head. 'No. What question did you ask me?'

Cara floundered. It had been much easier to ask him when it was dark and foggy and she couldn't see his lovely blue-grey eyes, but face to face, she was not quite as brave.

'I . . . I've probably got this wrong, but I thought I saw you going through Mr Anderson's pockets, but it was foggy and dark, so . . . '

He sat back in his chair and took a sip of his beer. She had the feeling that Guy was as nervous about this discussion as she was. 'I need to go back a long time to tell this story, Cara. But I also need to be clear that it's off the record.' He scoffed a little. 'I'm an idiot to be telling a journalist this. Do I have your word it won't go any further?'

'Yes, of course.'

Guy knew he must be mad to be telling Cara the truth about himself, but he wanted her to know. She was looking at him with such trusting eyes, yet he had given her no cause to trust him. He had indeed rifled Carl Anderson's pockets, but he had a good reason. At least to his mind he did. Would she agree? Or would she go running straight to the police? He had told the truth about his reasons for being there, but not about rummaging through Anderson's pockets.

'The story I told you today, about my life, was a lie. Well, parts of it were true, but mostly it was a lie. I do indeed own a sheep farm, but I only bought it a few years ago. We were never sheep farmers, nor were we really Australian.'

'I don't understand,' said Cara. She had put her head in her hands, listening to him so intently that it made him want to take one of her hands and kiss it. Any moment now her look of rapt attention would change to one of distaste. He had seen it before.

'This is where I have to go further back. My family were originally from Berlin.'

'So you're a German,' said Cara. To his amazement and relief she did not look horrified.

'Yes, I am. In the late nineteen-thirties, my father could see the way things were going in Germany and he didn't like it. He was a professor at the university in Berlin and saw his friends, good, noble, honest men, carried off to concentration camps. So my father took the decision to emigrate to Australia. We were fine for the first year or so. My father even gave speeches, speaking out against Hitler and his policies. Then war came.' Guy well remembered the mistrust to which his family were subjected. 'We were taken to an internment camp in Australia. I can't say we were treated badly, though I can't say we were treated well. We certainly didn't suffer as badly as my father's Jewish friends, so I try not to feel too bitter about it. But I was only ten years old when war broke out and I was sixteen before it ended properly and we were set free. I missed so much of my youth. All the things boys are supposed to do, like climbing trees, riding bikes, school dances. All that sort of thing.'

'I'm so sorry. It must have been awful for you.'

Guy marvelled that she had not run away from him. The war had cast a long shadow across Britain, and Germans were not popular. Brits especially distrusted those who had lived through the war and had apparently done nothing to speak out against Hitler. Perhaps she was just being kind and after this would have nothing more to do with him.

'It wasn't the best upbringing, that's true, but I wasn't alone and I do understand the reasons, even if I — and my family — suffered for them.'

'What happened to your family?' asked Cara. 'You never mention them in interviews.'

'My father died a year after we left the camp. It damn near destroyed him to be there, and he never truly recovered. My mother is still alive, but very elderly, so she can't travel — I was a late baby and my sister, Greta, was twenty years older than me. She's the reason I'm here. Before the war, she married a soldier. They were separated when my father decided to leave Germany. Greta wanted to stay with her husband, but she was having a baby. So my parents, and her friends, persuaded her it would be safer to get out of Germany.'

'Where are they now? Greta and the child, I mean?'

'My niece, Brigitte is fine. At least now.' Guy took another sip of his beer. Brigitte was a whole other problem. 'Greta? I don't know. That's why I employed Anderson. He was a private investigator. After the war, Greta naturally wanted to find her husband. We'd had no word of him for years. She managed to get work on a ship coming to Europe. She couldn't take Brigitte with her as the journey was too long, but she hoped to be reunited with her husband, and then arrange for Brigitte to join them. For reasons I'm not quite sure about, the last place she was seen is here, in Midchester. That was around November nineteen-forty-six. Nearly twenty years ago.'

'Is that why you asked me if I remembered what the figure on the bonfire looked like?'

Guy shut his eyes, not really wanting to think about it. 'After she left, we got a couple of postcards from her, then nothing. I fear that something happened to her. Why here, in this place, I don't understand. And now you're wondering why it took so long for me to come and find her?'

'No . . . Well a little bit, I suppose.'

'I couldn't afford it. I was only sixteen at the time and had missed much of my schooling, apart from what my mother and father managed to teach me and other children in the internment camp. So I didn't have a trade I could offer a ship. Besides, someone had to stay and provide for my mother and my niece. Mama was too old to work, and Brigitte too young. So I did any work I could for a few years. Then ten years ago, something awful happened. Brigitte ran away. She was only fifteen, but she managed to marry some sailor and she left Australia. I had to go looking for her first.'

'And you found her in America.'

'Good guess. Yes, she was in Los Angeles. The first husband had long gone by the time I found her. She'd married again, to a man who treated her as badly as the first one. I managed to get her out of that situation. Somehow, acting as her minder, I fell into acting in films too. And the rest as they say is history.'

'Guy, I don't know why you don't tell people the truth. This is a fascinating story. Much more interesting and less hackneyed than the tale you do tell. Sorry . . . ' Cara looked abashed. 'I don't mean to be rude.'

'It's like I said, Cara. Germans aren't popular at the moment and they were even less popular in the aftermath of the war. So I changed my name to one that sounded Australian and matched the accent I'd picked up along the way. Then, as I say, I let things slide. My niece was safe, relatively speaking. I don't think she'll ever truly be safe until she learns to stop picking men who abuse her. I was building up a career and making enough money to send back to my mother, until I had enough to ensure her safe and comfortable passage to Hollywood. But her first question when she got off the boat is 'Why have you stopped looking for Greta?' So here I am.'

'You employed Mr Anderson to find her?'

'Yes, and now he's dead. And in answer to your question as to why I rifled through his pockets, I hoped he had something for me. If he did, I didn't find it. I know I shouldn't have done it, but the fact of him dying in such a violent way suggests there's something going on here. I fear for Greta more than I ever did.'

'I'm so sorry,' said Cara, putting her small hand over his.

'Really?' Guy asked. 'You're not

running scared because I'm a big bad German?'

'Oh, that's old news,' she said,with a smile. 'Besides, I know what it's like to be judged because of your ancestry.'

'Really? How?'

'Now it's my turn for my life story.'

'I'm all ears,' said Guy.

'Before we moved to Midchester, Mum and Dad were travellers. Our whole family were gypsies. When my dad enlisted, Mum settled here. She was having me at the time, and said it had become hard to move around Britain with the war on. The government certainly liked it better if you stayed in one place.

'My dad died only a few months after he enlisted, and just before I was born — I'm the youngest of five — but Mum stayed here anyway. The villagers never really accepted Mum or her children. I gather my elder siblings were a wild lot, having been brought up on the road, but there was no harm in them. Mum struggled to bring us up alone, and she'd never had to keep a proper house. So things were always a bit chaotic. She said that didn't go down well with the housewives of Midchester.'

Cara pulled a face. 'A couple of times she was reported to the authorities, because people thought we were neglected, but that's not true. The house might not have always been very tidy, and her sheets might not have passed muster with the local women, but I don't remember ever being hungry or cold or unloved.'

'Your mum sounds like a remarkable woman.'

'She is. She's wonderful, and so clever. Even though we all went to school, she taught us other things, about the world and the people in it. I'm sure I don't have to tell you; when you've suffered prejudice, you learn a lot about human nature. I think that's why she was so forgiving of Herbie.'

'Herbie?'

'Herbie Potter, my step-dad. He's the local postman. He did something really stupid in the war over some girl that he'd really liked. It was covered up rather than cause embarrassment, but I think Mum was sorry for him because the villagers wouldn't talk to him for a while. She knew how that felt.'

'Do you like him?'

'Yes, I suppose I love him. He's the only dad I've ever known.' Cara looked across the bar, towards the main room and lowered her voice. 'He can be a bit of a miserable old goat at times. A bit too quick to pass judgement, which is ironic really, given his own history.' She shrugged and grimaced again.

'He who is without sin, eh?'

'Exactly.' Cara smiled.

Guy thought he could happily sit and look at her smile all day. The women he had known in the past were often very complicated. There was nothing complicated about Cara, even though she clearly felt things deeply. He couldn't help but notice the pain in her eyes when she talked about how her family were the target of prejudice by the villagers. But she seemed to accept it all without malice. She seemed to accept him too.

Dare he hope that he could find happiness in this village?

5

1946

It's hard to believe I've been happy here. I don't think I realised just how happy until she arrived and I was threatened with losing it all.

Here I carry on the fight on my own terms, because one day I know we will be victorious again. It is just a matter of being in the right place at the right time.

Midchester may not seem that important, but the information I was able to gain about the airfield during the war was vital to the Higher Command. It is just outside of Midchester, and now is only used for light chartered flights. But during the war it was overrun with American soldiers, who would tell you anything after a few drinks. What's more, you could tell them anything and they would believe you, so it was easy to spread misinformation that threatened their morale.

I may not have been able to fight in real terms, but I helped the cause in my own way. At the same time I earned the villager's respect. I don't say that they like me. I'm not a likeable person and never have been, but they admire the things I do.

How can I give all that up? If I'm found out, I'll go to prison and they'll hang me.

Even if I manage to get away, how can I return to the Fatherland as it is now, occupied by allied troops?

Every day I have feared them finding the papers that might implicate me in espionage. Better to be here, where I can easily take flight if needs be, than to go straight into the lion's den.

If she is here too, people will start asking questions, such as why I am close to a German girl after all they did in the war.

She dreams of us being a real family. I know that will never happen, not in the current climate. The only way to do that would be to leave and reinvent myself yet again.

I cannot do that. I will not do that. Not when I am so close to success at last.

How does one kill the thing one loves most in the world?

* * *

1966

'What do you think of this?' said Peg Bradbourne, coming into the pub a few evenings later. She threw a newspaper on the bar and hopped on her stool. 'Another murder in Midchester. The villagers are torn between fascination and horror.'

Cara, who was polishing glasses, stopped what she was doing to get Peg's bottle of stout, and then looked at the paper. It reported on the results of the coroner's report.

'There's nothing to be fascinated about. Poor Mr Anderson.'

'Yes, it is rather sad for such a young man. And it's — frightening to think we have a killer in our midst. Talking of young men, how is your young man? You know everyone is gossiping now about him being German.'

Cara bit back a retort that Guy was not her young man, but only because she liked Peg. 'Yes, I heard Mrs Simpson and one of her friends on about it in the mini market this morning.'

'But you already knew?'

'He told me the other night. Honestly, Peg, what does it matter? The war was twenty years ago. People should move on.'

'Sadly those in Midchester have long memories, as you well know, dear. They're also inclined to turn on people very quickly. There was that old professor, Solomon his name was. They thought that he . . . ' Peg stopped. 'I'm sorry, Cara. You probably already know all this.'

'No, I don't. What?'

'Well when Herbie was bein . . . shall we say, naughty? They thought Professor Solomon was a German saboteur. He had a heart attack while in custody. He did recover, thankfully, but he was never the same afterwards. He was a Jew who already lost all his family in the camps. Being suspected of spying in Midchester broke his spirit, I think.'

'It's not right, Peg. I understand it was the war and everyone was afraid, what with the bombing and everything, but to hound an innocent man like that, it's awful. I didn't know about it, because Mum and Herbie never told me. All I can say is that Mum is far more forgiving than I am.'

'I doubt that sweetheart. You seem to have forgiven Mr Sullivan for being German.'

'But he hasn't done anything, Peg. The sins of the father should never be visited upon the child.'

'I know this, dear girl. I'm just making an observation.'

'Sorry, Peg. I just feel so strongly about this. I know what it's like to have the whole village against you.'

'Not the whole village, Cara.'

'No, I know. I'm sorry, I didn't mean to include you in that. You were always kind to us, and so was Mr Yeardley who used to own the pub. His daughter, Betty, used to babysit for my mum sometimes.'

'They're good people.'

'You're good people, Peg.'

Cara had to move away to serve customers. It was getting busy and there was no sign of Nancy, who had gone out again.

'Where's Nancy?' asked Peg, when Cara had a moment.

'I don't know. She's not usually like this. She never misses an opening or closing time. But lately she just keeps going off and it's as if she's forgotten about the pub. I don't like to say anything, because she is the boss, and she's been so good to me. I shouldn't even be complaining about her now.'

'Maybe I can help,' said a voice from the bar. Cara turned to see Guy standing there. He was dressed in jeans, with a black roll neck sweater that clung to his muscular arms and defined his torso to disturbing effect.

'What? Sorry, hello, Mr Sullivan.'

'I thought we'd agreed it was Guy.'

Had they? Cara couldn't remember, but she was happy enough to call him by his first name. Only then did it occur to her to wonder what his real German name was. She would really like to know.

'What can I get you?' she asked.

'I meant it, Cara. Let me help. I've worked in a bar before, in Australia. That's if you're not afraid to be seen fraternising with the enemy.' He winked and Cara could not help but smile.

'I couldn't let you help,' she protested. 'You're a customer.'

'And the customer is always right, so

let me help you.'

'Oh go on,' said Peg, 'Let him help. Hello, Mr Sullivan. We haven't been introduced. I'm Peg Bradbourne.'

Guy stretched across the bar and shook Peg's hand. 'Pleased to meet you, Miss Bradbourne.'

'Oh now, let's not be formal. I'm Peg and you're Guy. And I can tell you that I have no problems about fraternising with the enemy when he's as handsome as you are.'

'It looks like you're out-voted,' Guy said to Cara.

'It seems so.' She lifted the hatch and let him behind the bar. 'I'll show you where everything is.'

'Don't worry, I know my way around a pub. I'll soon find everything. You just go and serve the customers.'

The clientele who came in after that all did a double take when they saw Guy behind the bar. It also made it harder for them to gossip about him, because at any time he could be clearing glasses off the table.

'That's Mrs Simpson coming in,' Cara told Guy. Len Simpson had arrived earlier in the evening. 'She drinks lemonade. The lady with her drinks gin and tonic. Oh and here's their other friend. She likes a vodka and lime.'

'How do you remember all this?' Guy asked her.

'Because I've been working here for five years and no-one has ever asked for anything different.'

'Really? Let's see if we can shake this up a little. We'll put some cocktails on the menu.'

'I don't know, Guy,' said Cara, doubtfully. 'Nancy has tried that before, and they tend to get a bit shirty about her bringing in new-fangled ideas.'

'Come on, live a little. You got any champagne?'

'I . . . yes, I think Nancy keeps a bottle for special occasions.'

'Right, let's perk this place up a bit. I'll find the vermouth and other ingredients. You get the champagne.'

‘I’m not sure anyone will drink cocktails. I hear there was a riot the first time someone suggested adding lime to lager. That was in the nineteenth century, I think, and we’re only just getting the blood out of the carpet.’

‘They’ll like them when they see how I make one.’

Peg grinned at Cara and nodded her head in encouragement.

When Cara returned to the bar with the champagne, she found Guy doing incredible things with bottles, spinning them over his head and then squirting short bursts of each into glasses. He added the champagne, then as an extra flourish, he had managed to find some sparklers that were put aside for Bonfire night and he put one in each glass. Some of the customers were standing up, fascinated by the show.

‘Who’s going to be first to try my champagne cocktail?’ Guy raised an eyebrow, but there did not seem to be any takers.

‘Me,’ said Peg. ‘I want one of those.’

'OK then, as you're the first, this one is on me,' said Guy, putting the cocktail in front of her. 'I'd wait 'til the sparkler has gone out, if I were you.'

Peg did as she was asked, and then took a sip. The whole pub seemed to be holding its breath. 'Hmm, delicious,' she said. There was a collective sigh of relief, almost as if they had all been afraid the drink would blow up in Peg's face.

'Great,' said Guy. 'Who's next?'

After that, all the ladies wanted to try one, even the normally tea-total Mrs Simpson. The men muttered something about the drinks being too girly for them, but they did enjoy watching Guy make them. Someone put the jukebox on, and the atmosphere changed considerably as the sound of the Beatles singing *Love Me Do* filled the room.

'I'm afraid to ask what sort of gin joints you worked in,' Cara laughed, feeling suddenly carefree.

Guy winked at her and said, 'Yeah, you probably don't want to know. We're out of meat pies. Where do you keep them?'

'I'll get them, you just keep twirling bottles. It's positively hypnotising the men. I've never seen them so docile. You'll have to teach me how to do it.'

* * *

Guy waited until Cara had gone out back for the pies, then put the bottle down. With the pub so noisy, it would be easier for him to chat to Peg. 'I hear you're the one in the know around here,' he said to her.

'I like to keep my eyes and ears open,' said Peg. She hiccoughed slightly. 'Really, Guy, these cocktails are lethal. If I find out you've used one to corrupt that lovely girl in there . . . '

'I'd never do that to Cara,' said Guy. 'Scouts honour.'

'I'm glad to hear it. What is it you want to know?'

'Do you remember back to the war years, Peg?'

'My dear boy, I remember it clearly. I'm not sure about what happened yesterday morning, but the war is stuck in my head.'

'Of course, I'm sorry. I just wondered if, after the war, around the time of that first bonfire party, you'd seen a young German woman around these parts.'

'I don't remember doing so. Do you have a picture?'

Guy took his wallet from his pocket and found the picture of Greta. 'Here she is. My sister, Greta.'

'She's a very pretty girl.'

'Yes, she is . . . I mean she was.'

'You think she's dead?'

'I'm afraid she might be. I can't imagine she'd abandon her family and her daughter.'

Guy had thought about it time and time again. Greta had been a devoted mother, and had sobbed on the day they waved her off on the ship, leaving little Brigitte with Guy and their mother. She would not just decide to stay away from those she loved.

'What was she doing in Midchester?'

'That's a good question, Peg. I don't know. She left Australia to come back to Europe, hoping to find her husband after the war. I know she went to Berlin, because we got a postcard from there. I also know she spent some time in Hamburg. She sent us a postcard from there too, saying that she was getting closer to finding her husband, Frederick.' He pronounced it 'Free-drick'. 'Carl Anderson somehow tracked her down to Midchester, but he didn't give me full details. He just told me to meet him here.'

Peg had been looking intently at the photograph as Guy spoke. She shook her head, sadly.

'I'm sorry, Guy, but I don't remember this girl. If she was here, it won't have been long enough to make an impression.'

'You'd think people would notice a German girl around here, so soon after the war.'

'Well, yes, I agree. That's why it's

strange that I don't remember her. Ask some of the others. The Simpsons were living here then, as was Herbie Potter and his wife, Cara's mum.' Peg swivelled on her stool and turned to where Mrs Simpson sat with her friends. 'Myrtle, come here a moment.'

Mrs Simpson got up and walked unsteadily to the bar. She gave a loud hiccough on the way. 'What is it, Ma Cherry?'

Guy and Peg exchanged amused glances. 'We need your help, ma cherie,' said Peg, gently correcting her. 'Do you remember seeing this young lady around here, just after the war? Her name was Greta.' Peg looked to Guy for clarification.

At the same time, Cara had returned with the pies. Guy saw her look of curiosity and waved her over.

'I'm just doing some investigating of my own,' he explained. He turned back to Mrs Simpson. 'Her maiden name was Greta Mueller, but she married a man called Frederick Schwartz. She could have been using either name when she came here. Her passport was still in her maiden name because there'd been no chance to change it when we left Germany.'

Mrs Simpson peered at the picture. Guy wished he had not sold her that cocktail, as he wasn't certain she was in a fit state to remember anything. 'You're very handsome, for a German,' she said, gazing up at Guy.

'You're not bad for a British woman,' Guy said, then immediately wished he hadn't when he heard Cara's sudden intake of breath. It was a cheap shot, but he was in no mood to be patronised.

'Hmm,' Mrs Simpson giggled, as his rebuke went over her head. 'I think you're just trying to get me drunk so you can get information from me.'

'Good guess,' he said. 'I'm trying to find out what happened to my sister.'

Mrs Simpson looked at the picture again. 'I do remember something. You were ill that week, Peg, don't you remember? You couldn't get to the bonfire party.'

'Oh yes, I remember now. I had the flu and took to my bed.'

'By the time you were up and about it was all over.'

'What was all over?'

'This girl was looking for someone. Oh what was the name?'

'Frederick Schwartz? He was Greta's husband.'

'Was he? That might have been it then. But we had no Germans here. There was that old Professor Solomon . . .'

'He was Polish,' said Peg.

'Yes I remember now. And his daughter, Rachel. Sullen girl.'

'They were Jews,' Peg explained to Guy. 'They'd suffered quite a lot.'

'I can imagine. My father lost a lot of his friends that way.'

'Anyway,' said Mrs Simpson, seeming annoyed because Peg was taking all of Guy's attention, 'One day the girl was here, asking about someone, and the next day she was gone. Only . . . There was something else. Something in the paper. I can't remember what it was now.' She put her hand to her head. 'I'm going to have such a headache in the morning. You really are a very naughty boy, serving those cocktails, Mr Sullivan.'

'I bet you've never had so much fun though.'

'Well . . . ' Mrs Simpson burst into a fit of girlish giggles. 'You really are naughty. If I were thirty years younger, I'd set my cap at you. You watch yourself, Cara. A man like this can have any woman he wants. And you've had problems with men before.'

'I can take care of myself,' Cara said quietly. Guy wondered what problems she had with other men, but he had other concerns at that moment.

'Do you remember anything else?' he asked Mrs Simpson.

'Not just now. If I do remember anything, I'll let you know.'

'Thank you, Mrs Simpson. You've been really helpful. Now, perhaps you'll let me buy you another drink.'

'Best make it lemonade,' said Peg firmly, raising a disapproving eyebrow.

'Oh, no, I want another cocktail.'

'Leave it to me,' said Guy. He went and played with the bottles as he had before, then put a sparkling cocktail down on the bar in front of her.

Mrs Simpson walked away with it, still unsteady on her feet.

'Do you think that was wise?' asked Cara.

Guy leant in and whispered to her, getting a delicious waft of her sunflower shampoo as he did so and her silky hair brushed his face. 'It's lemonade and lime, with a dash of orange juice. She'll be fine.'

Cara laughed. 'She'll be having us under the Trade Descriptions Act.'

'She'll wake up tomorrow and be none the wiser, though she may have less of a headache. Come on, let's do some more cocktails.' Guy wanted to ask more questions of the other villagers, but he realised it was a bad idea to push it. At the moment they seemed to accept him, because he had brought a little sparkle into their lives. Too many reminders of his origins might put an end to that. He had won over the women, but the men were going to be harder.

'Cara,' he said, remembering something else.

'Yes?'

'I've been invited to Mr Black's house tomorrow night for the big dinner party he's throwing. I wasn't going to go, but maybe we could ask him questions, him owning the newspaper and all that. I can take a guest. Would you like to come with me?'

'I don't know, Guy. Nancy is off doing other things at the moment, and I'm really busy here.'

'So tell her you deserve a night off.'

'Yes, I could do that, I suppose. But I already have one night off a week for my journalism class. That's on Friday.'

'Please ask. I'd like to take you.' Guy could not understand why it mattered to him so much that she say yes. Cara was far too distracting. Once again he told himself to be careful he did not get side-tracked.

'OK,' she said. 'I'll see what I can do.'

'Great! If it's OK, give me a call at the Grange and I'll pick you up at seven.'

The next hour or so was filled with Guy making cocktails for everyone. A lot of the ladies wanted one just like the last one Mrs Simpson had. It was just as well — they were out of champagne now.

'I've never seen everyone so happy,' said Cara as the jukebox started up again and the Rolling Stones' *Not Fade Away* filled the bar-room. 'Though I don't think I could cope with this every night.'

'Nah, you want quiet times too. But this is good. Everyone is enjoying themselves and they're spending money.'

'Show us how you throw those bottles again,' one of the male customers called to Guy.

Guy picked up two bottles and started juggling with them. It was something he used to do in Australia. A bit of showmanship that encouraged people to spend more money. The customers applauded him, and he realised he was having a good time, despite the circumstances.

He also realised he was showing off outrageously. Part of him wanted to impress Cara, and judging by the way she laughed at his antics, she was very impressed.

'Show me how you do it,' she said, at last.

'OK. Put one bottle in each hand. The first trick is to spin them over without spilling a drop.'

'I'll never manage that.'

'Of course you will. It's the rule of centrifugal force.'

'The what?'

'I don't know, really. I just made that up. But if you do it quickly enough, the liquid doesn't spill. Come on, show me.'

Cara flicked one of the bottles over. Instead of her catching it, it fell to the floor, shattering. That made all the customers laugh and applaud.

'Well done, Cara,' several of them called.

Her face was a picture and Guy had to suppress his own laughter because she looked so forlorn.

Suddenly the door of the pub slammed, silencing everyone. The atmosphere changed in an instant, from cheerful to wary.

Nancy walked to the centre of the room, her face a mask of fury. 'What on Earth is going on in my pub?'

6

1946

Who would have thought such an idiot could be so much help? All I had to do is supply him with drink, guessing that he will one day end up with the same weakness as his vile mother. A few glasses of brandy and he will tell me all about the prank he pulled with his friends. It might have won them first prize at the Guy Fawkes contest if he had not had a fit of the giggles. I won't have to worry about that happening.

He has lank brown hair and spotty skin. Not your perfect Aryan male, but you have to work with what you've got. At seventeen, he's like all the boys who just missed joining in the war effort. All talk about the heroic things he might have done.

'I'd have shown Hitler,' he says,

taking a sip of brandy. He wrinkles his nose. Maybe he's not like his mother.

'Go on, be a man and drink up,' I urge.

He swallows the booze down and for a moment I fear he's going to vomit all over the carpet.

'I hear you're seeing young Nancy,' I say. 'They tell me she's a bit of a goer.'

He looks taken aback at that. 'She's a nice girl,' he says. 'I know she flirts a bit, but she never means it, and she doesn't mess around with other blokes.'

'Oh no, of course not. I wasn't suggesting anything of the sort. But if I were a bit younger . . . '

'You wouldn't?' He grins, excitement lighting up his eyes. Men always like to think their girl is irresistible to others.

'I would.'

'Yeah, well I do and often,' he smirks. I know then that he's lying. Nancy probably is a good girl at heart. But I play along, pandering to his ego.

'I bet you do, Tiger. Have another drink.' I pour another glass of brandy down him, and sit next to him on the sofa. He moves up a little, clearly disturbed by my proximity. We're at my place, away from anywhere we might be overheard. Peg Bradbourne has got over whatever it was that kept her away from the pub, so I need to be extra careful.

'Show me how you did the Guy Fawkes thing,' I demand. 'I want to play a trick on some friends.'

'I'll need newspapers and some old trousers and a sweater. Oh and a big paper bag.'

This is where I have to be really clever. The boy might talk, and I need to make sure he doesn't. 'I don't suppose you could go and get some of your mother's old clothes. And some newspaper and a bag. I used up my last lot to build the fire.'

When he looks doubtful, I say, 'Go on, get them. There's a fiver in it for you.' I pull a five pound note from my pocket and wave it in front of his greedy little eyes.

I know his mother spends all her

money on booze. As a result the boy always looks half-starved. It won't take long to get him drunk on an empty stomach. But I need him sober enough to bring the things, so I hold back on the drink for a while and send him out into the night. I'm afraid he might not return, but he does, no doubt lured by the thought of a five pound note. Then he takes me through the process.

'It takes at least two people,' he says. 'One to be the Guy, and the other to stuff the newspapers in and put the paper bag over the head. Just cut out holes for the eyes, nose and mouth. Oh yeah, I forgot. You'll need gloves as well, to hide the hands.'

'I can get some,' I tell him. I won't really need them, because no-one else will see my creation. At least not until it's too late, and by then, the body and clothing will be burned beyond recognition.

'Thanks, Sammy,' I tell him as I let him back out into the night. He's swaying a little.

'My fiver . . . ' he says.

Oh, so he's not that drunk then.

'Of course, it's well-earned too.'

I give him the five pounds. It's a forgery, left over from the war. I'd managed to slip them into the local economy, causing a panic for a short time. But it doesn't take people long to become apathetic about such things, so I doubt anyone will notice.

'Get yourself some chips on the way home. And remember, not a word to anyone.'

'My lips are sealed,' he says, before hiccoughing and walking away, clutching the five pound note. I want to tell him to be careful or the colours will run before he has time to spend it, but what does it matter if they do?

If he ever says anything to anyone, I can tell them that he turned up drunk, insisting he show me the trick. I'll deny all knowledge of the five pound note. It'll be his word against mine. With the reputation he has for trouble, I think they'll all believe me.

* * *

1966

Breakfast at The Quiet Woman was a tense affair. Nancy barely spoke to Cara. She sat with her face behind a newspaper. Normally, they would chat about the evening before. That was obviously a sore subject, after Nancy arrived to see Cara dropping an expensive bottle of spirits onto the floor. Not even Guy's offer to pay for it had softened her heart.

'Will you be using the car today, Nancy?' Cara asked, as she poured Rice Crispies into the bowl. The Hilman Minx belonged to Nancy, so Cara never used it without permission.

'I might be.'

'Oh, OK.'

Cara poured milk on her cereal. There was barely any left, so it emptied the bottle.

'That's just like you, isn't it?' Nancy

put her newspaper down onto the table with a thwack. 'Using the last of the milk. Honestly, Cara, why don't you think?'

'I'll go and get some more.' Cara's face burned scarlet. She felt like a recalcitrant child. She had never known Nancy to treat her this way. Running out of milk was a regular occurrence and neither of them ever blamed the other. Pushing her cereals away, she got up and went to get her coat.

'So are you just going to waste this cereal and milk now?'

Cara turned back. 'Look, Nancy, I said I'm sorry about last night. And I'm sorry about the milk and I'm sorry because I can't do anything to please you at the moment. But I was on my own last night because you had gone off without warning . . . again. Guy just stepped in to help.'

'No-one goes behind that bar without my say so. Least of all some big-headed Hollywood star who thinks he can just come here and show off. I'm the boss here. Something you seem to be forgetting.'

'Well, as I'm obviously annoying you at the moment, perhaps it's best if you're not my boss anymore. As soon as I can, I'll get my things and leave!'

'I think that's the best idea you've had all morning. I obviously can't trust you to run the pub alone! Honestly, Cara, what were you thinking?'

Cara grabbed her coat and stormed out. Nancy was her dearest friend. They had spent so many good times together working behind the bar, and normally enjoyed each other's company as flatmates. How had things got so bad so quickly?

Cara headed for the place she always went in time of need. The local shop. The owner, Mr Fletcher, smiled as she entered. He was an elderly man, who wore round glasses at the end of his nose. His body was just as round as the spectacles. 'Hello, Cara. Run out of milk again?'

'Yes, actually. But right now I just

want a bag of sweets.'

'Oh dear. It's one of those days, is it?'

She nodded glumly. 'Yes, it's definitely one of those days.'

'What can I tempt you with? We've got Sherbet Dib-dabs, white mice, Jelly Babies, rhubarb and custard, Black Jacks. Or what about your favourites, coconut mushrooms?' Mr Fletcher gestured behind the counter, like a magician drawing a rabbit from a hat. There had always been a bit of the showman in him.

Behind him, glass jars gleamed on polished mahogany shelves; a rainbow of different sweets to suit each palate. When Cara was a little girl it could take her up to half an hour to decide what she wanted, but Mr Fletcher had never rushed her then and he didn't rush her now. Not like the sullen kohl-eyed girl with badly back-combed and black rooted hair in the mini-market who glared at you if you didn't just pick and pay for what you wanted.

Remembering that she was no longer

a child and couldn't really take all day to decide, Cara said, 'If I give you a shilling, can you mix them up for me, please?'

'Goodness, I haven't done a mix for you since you were a little girl. It must be bad.'

She nodded again, but did not want to tell him, even though he seemed eager to find out. She liked Mr Fletcher, but she knew from past experience that every bit of gossip was passed onto the next customer, who passed it on to everyone they knew. As angry as she was with Nancy, she was not prepared to criticise her to the whole of Midchester.

Not that last night would be a secret. Everyone in the pub had seen Nancy's reaction to the cocktails and the loud jukebox. Cara flushed again, recalling how humiliated she felt.

Mr Fletcher measured the sweets out onto the scales. Cara knew without a doubt that he had thrown in a few extra. That was something else you couldn't get at the mini-market. All the sweets there were pre-wrapped and by the time you took the packaging off there were very few left. They didn't taste the same either.

Taking her sweets, Cara walked along the main street, chewing on a Black Jack. They were not the healthiest of breakfasts, but they did taste good. The delicious aniseed flavouring coated her tongue black. As she passed some children on their way to school, she poked it out at them, making them burst out laughing. She was not surprised when she looked back and saw them running into Mr Fletcher's shop.

She wandered up to her mum's house. Cara opened the gate and walked round to the back of the house where Martha Potter was putting clothes on the line. 'Hello, love, you're out early.'

'Mum.' Clutching her sweets in her hand, Cara's eyes filled with tears. She realised she must look just like a child, especially with running home to mummy. 'Mum . . . '

'Sweetheart, what is it?' Martha held open loving arms to her daughter. 'Has someone been saying something to you?'

Cara nodded, and then shook her head. 'Yes, no, I don't know. I packed in my job then Nancy sacked me anyway.'

'Herbie told me what happened in the pub last night. I don't know what's come over Nancy.' She took Cara by the arm. 'Come on in and I'll put the kettle on. And you can put those sweets away, young lady. I'll make you a proper breakfast.'

Ten minutes later Cara sat at the small Formica table in the cluttered kitchen, while the aroma of bacon frying on the Baby Belling cooker filled the air. 'Do you want an egg, love?' asked Martha.

'I don't know if I can eat anything.'

'You managed a Black Jack,' her mother said, disapprovingly. 'This will be much better for you.' Martha cracked an egg into the pan where it sizzled and spat. This was how Cara always remembered it. If anything went wrong, even during the war when there was rationing, — Martha would cook up a filling meal. Their favourite comfort food had been bread pudding. Cara wished she had some of that now.

'Hello, what's this?' said Herbie, coming into the kitchen. He was on his rounds, but as Len Simpson had told everyone at the pub, he always stopped off at home for a cup of tea and a bacon sandwich.

'Cara hasn't got a job anymore, love. It means she'll have to come home.'

'Oh, I see.'

'No!' Cara protested. She had not even thought of that. She wanted to be an independent young woman and she couldn't do that with her mum fussing over her. 'I don't want to intrude on you and Herbie.' She could tell from Herbie's look he agreed with her, but then he looked at her mother's resolute face.

'Of course she should come home if that's what you want, love,' he said. 'You're family, Cara.'

'Thank you, Herbie, but you don't really want me around.'

'We'll not have that talk,' he said. 'I've known you since you were a baby. You might not be my flesh and blood, but as far as I'm concerned you're my daughter. What happened with Nancy?'

Cara was reluctant to say, knowing that as the local postman, Herbie could gossip as much as Mr Fletcher in the sweet shop.

'I was in the pub last night,' he said. 'I know what went on, with all the cocktails and Nancy turning up and shouting at everyone. I thought she'd have got over that by this morning.'

'Well she didn't,' said Cara. 'So I lost my temper and told her I was leaving.' She felt the tears rising again. 'Then she said it was just as well and she was sacking me anyway. I'll have to go and look for another job.'

Martha put a plate of bacon and eggs

in front of her. 'You're not leaving here until you've eaten that breakfast.'

'Any bacon left for me, love?' Herbie looked hopeful.

'No, you'll just have to have an egg sandwich this morning.'

'Oh.' Herbie sat opposite Cara, eyeing her bacon longingly. When her mother had put an egg sandwich in front of Herbie, then went off to do some housework, Cara took one of her slices of bacon and put it in his sandwich.

'Thanks, pet. A sandwich isn't right without a bit of bacon.'

'I won't impose on you, Herbie, I promise. It didn't work the last time I lived at home.' As Cara had gotten older, the little house had suffocated her. She was ashamed to remember that she had taken it out on Herbie. For a while their relationship had been very strained.

She felt an added pang remembering that she had turned up on Nancy's doorstep, crying and saying she had nowhere to live. The pub landlady had taken her in and given her a job. And now she had thanked Nancy by storming out because they had run out of milk.

But that was not all of it. Nancy had never been so angry with her, not even in the first few weeks of Cara's employment when she dropped enough glasses and bottles to stock the entire pub. Something had happened to her friend, and Cara's only response was to run away, instead of sticking around to see if she could help. She despised herself for letting Nancy down.

Herbie took a deep breath. 'I'm not going to see you out on the street, lass. Besides, you're grown up now, and I'm not as finicky as I used to be.' He put up his hand to halt her protests. 'No, I admit, I like things a certain way, but I soon realised that it was putting too much strain on your mother. I don't want her to think I'm a tyrant.'

'You're not a tyrant, Herbie. You

never have been. You've been good to all of us.'

Cara ate what she could of her breakfast, and then went to find her mother. In the middle of dusting, Martha had sat down in one of the big armchairs to read a book, with the duster still in one hand.

'Oh, I was just finishing this off,' she said, smiling up at her daughter. 'She thinks he hates her, but of course he doesn't. He's just trying to look out for his brother, who's the black sheep of the family.'

Cara sat in the other armchair and curled her legs under her. The room was as she always remembered it, with every surface piled high with books. Most of them were romances, but there were also dozens of classics. Some of the books were stained with the brown rings of a thousand cups of tea. When Herbie first moved in with them, he had tried to restore order, even alphabetising the bookcase. But neither Martha nor her children were used to putting them back, so he admitted defeat.

Cara pulled a book from the nearest pile and opened it.

As she and her mother read their books, Cara realised how much she missed being home, despite longing to be independent. There was no pressure to be anything other than herself. It would be nice to be back, but she also knew that after a while she would get the wanderlust again. It was in her blood.

Herbie called to say he was going back to work. An hour passed with Cara and Martha reading in comfortable silence. Then there was a light knock on the sitting room door.

'Hello, sorry.'

It was Guy, dressed in black trousers and a thick Astrakhan coat. It was open a little at the top, revealing a tie-dyed t-shirt.

He was the last person she had expected to see in this house. Cara jumped up, dropping her book on the floor. She looked around, immediately wishing that her mum could be a little bit tidier.

'I did knock on the back door,' said Guy, 'but there was no answer. It was open so . . . '

'Oh that's fine,' said Cara. 'People just tend to come and go as they please in this house.'

'I went to the pub to find you, but Nancy said . . . '

Cara nodded. Lost in her book, she had almost forgotten her problems. 'I quit. I think. It's all a bit confusing.'

'Cara, I'm so sorry. This is all my fault,' Guy said.

'No, it isn't.' Cara realised her mum was watching them both questioningly. 'Oh . . . sorry, you've met my mum, haven't you?'

'I have indeed. It's nice to meet you again, Mrs Baker.'

'Potter.'

'Of course, I apologise.'

'That's alright, Mr Sullivan. Would you like a cup of tea?'

'Actually I was wondering if I could borrow Cara for a while. I thought she might be able to help me with something.'

'Is it to do with your sister?' Cara asked.

Guy nodded. 'Yep, I want to find out what Anderson knew.'

'Oh,' said Martha Potter. 'That reminds me. I'm very sorry for my behaviour the other night, Mr Sullivan. The slanging match with Mrs Simpson wasn't right with that poor man bleeding to death in the street.'

'Please, forget about it. I can tell from your lovely daughter that you're a decent woman.'

Martha smiled and seemed to grow several inches. 'Well, you will have to excuse the mess. I was busy with housework, and then Cara turned up needing breakfast.'

Cara was about to protest, because the housework would not have been finished, breakfast or not, but decided against it. It would explain why the room was so untidy.

'Don't worry about it,' said Guy. 'Actually this makes me feel a bit homesick. Our house in Australia was always piled high with books. There was little room for anything else. There's nothing better in life than a well-loved, well-used book with tea-stains on the cover.'

Whether he told the truth or not, Cara blessed him for not making her mother feel embarrassed about the mess, though she inwardly cringed because he had noticed the tea-stains.

She gave herself a mental slap. Why should she feel ashamed of her mother and her home? Martha Potter was the very best of women, regardless of the state of her house. If Guy could not see that, then quite frankly it was his problem.

'I really like your mum,' he said, a few minutes later as they walked through Midchester.

'So do I,' said Cara, with a smile.

'I meant what I said about my house,

you know. We had loads of books.'

'Really? You weren't just being kind?'

'Not at all. It really did remind me of home. I'd have liked to have stayed longer, but I didn't want to intrude on your mum's reading schedule.'

'Now you're just teasing.'

'A little, maybe. But I still think she's great. She gave birth to you for a start, and that raises her high in my estimation.'

Cara did not know how to respond to that. 'So what do you want to do? About finding Greta?'

'I've been trying to retrace Carl Anderson's steps. I've been in touch with his office and they tell me that he visited Shrewsbury library. Do you have any idea why he might do that?'

'They keep all the local history books there, and old newspapers. They've got some old family records too.'

'But my family wouldn't be recorded there.'

'No, but perhaps Greta's husband is listed on the local electoral register.'

'I never thought of that. But he'd hardly use his real name. Not around here, and not just after the war ended.'

'Maybe he used a name that was very similar and Carl Anderson made the connection.'

'I knew you'd be good at this.'

'Oh come on, Guy, you don't really need my help.'

He took her hand in his. 'Actually I do. I like having you around. Is that OK with you?'

She beamed up at him. 'It's absolutely OK with me.' — 'Good, so we'll go to Shrewsbury and then we'll go to dinner at Mr Black's place tonight. Unless you're sick of me by then.'

'I won't be. Besides, while I'm in Shrewsbury I can look in the labour exchange for another job.'

'I will pay you.'

'What?' Cara glared at him.

'I didn't mean in that way. I meant as a researcher. You must be good at that, what with being a journalist. You did your research on me well.'

She didn't want to admit that all she had really done was remembered every single thing she had read about him in magazines over the years. 'I suppose so,' she said instead.

'Good, then I'll pay you for your time while you help me. I was paying Anderson fifteen pounds a day. Is that enough?'

'Fifteen pounds a day!' She gaped at him incredulously. 'I didn't earn that in a week at the pub.'

'Well, I can't pay you less than I paid him. It wouldn't be right, would it?'

'But the difference is that you'll be with me, so I'd only really be doing half the work, if that. Look, I'll accept fifteen pounds a week, and that's it.' It was a few pounds more than she earned at the pub, but she figured that being a researcher was a little higher up the employment scale than a barmaid.

Guy still seemed unhappy about it. 'You're never going to be rich this way, Cara.'

'I don't care about being rich. I just

care about doing an honest day's work for an honest day's pay.'

'OK, fifteen pounds a week it is. Plus expenses.'

'But . . . '

'No, buts, Cara. I'll pay all the out of pocket expenses as well. Agreed?'

'Agreed.' He held out his hand and she shook it.

Cara could not help feeling excited about working with Guy. She prayed that she could help him find his sister. In reality she believed that after twenty years the trail might have gone cold. Any news Anderson might have had would not be good and that was perhaps what cost him his life.

She gave Guy's hand a comforting squeeze.

'I know what you're thinking,' he said. He kissed her on the forehead, sending a frisson of excitement through her. 'I'm not going to get the happy reunion I'd like, but at least I'll know for sure and then my family can move on.'

She squeezed his hand again, relishing the feel of his skin against hers. 'We'll find her, Guy, I know we will.'

Whether they would find Greta alive was a different matter.

7

1946

Now the time has come I'm not sure if I can do it. She arrives to see me, so trusting, so loving; never seeing the danger that lies ahead. I'm struck again by how lovely she is. We used to dream about the time we could be together always. After all the planning, dreams and schemes, it tears at my heart to know that I'm going to have to make the rest of my journey through life without her.

'So this is where you live,' she says, looking around. 'Who would have imagined all those years ago in Berlin that we both would have come so far?' She seems suddenly shy. 'At least you've done well. I couldn't get decent work in Australia. I saved all I could to come and find you. Then I had to work on that awful ship, cleaning up other people's vomit. It was worth it to come here. I feared I'd never see you again.'

'You shouldn't have come,' I tell her savagely. 'You should have stayed with your daughter.' I can see the words are like a knife to her heart, but I want her to be angry with me; to fight back. It will make things easier.

'I know you're angry about Brigitte,' she says, 'but I thought I'd explained it to you at the time. I did what I had to do.'

'Why? Were you raped?'

She slumps down onto the sofa. 'You know exactly what I mean and don't pretend you don't. It was your idea! You said it was the only way I could escape from Germany with my family. Don't you remember?'

I remember, but I didn't think she would actually go through with it. it was a test of her love, and she failed me.

'You can be so cruel sometimes,' she tells me. 'Maybe it's better if I go away.

I can't see you ever taking to Brigitte and I can't just abandon her.'

I strike another blow to her heart. 'You already abandoned her to come here.'

She puts her head in her hands. 'Don't you think I know that? If I didn't love you so much, I wouldn't have done it. Isn't that enough for you? Isn't it proof of my love that I left my daughter in the care of my elderly mother and teenage brother for months upon end?'

'How is young Hans nowadays? He can't have been more than eight years old the last time I saw him.' I'd rather talk about him than Brigitte. The child reminds me of the betrayal.

She smiles indulgently. Her brother has always been her pride and joy. 'He's tall, handsome and easily passes for an Australian amongst people who don't know any different. He's picked up the accent very quickly. He's clever too. He could be anything he wanted to be, if only they would let him. Instead he has to work menial jobs, cleaning out public conveniences and helping to unload ships at the docks in Sidney. He's a good boy. A hard worker.'

'He should have been in Germany, fighting for the cause.'

She snorts. 'There's no way Papa would have let Hans join the Hitler Youth. Not everyone loves the Fuhrer as you did.'

'Do.'

'What?'

'Not everyone loves him as I do.'

'So you still believe in him, even after all that's happened? Can't you see that he was just an evil little man who caused untold suffering? Not just to the Jews and the gypsies and others he considered undesirable, but to his own people. No-one was safe while he was alive.'

I lean over and grab her by the shoulders.

'You're traitors, all of you.'

For God's sake, get angry, I silently scream at her. Shout at me. Attack me.

Make this easier.

'You, your father, your ridiculous mother and your brother. I can forgive him. He was just a child. You all brainwashed him.'

'If you hate me so much, I should just go.'

But I can't let her go. Not with what she knows. She'll return to Australia and tell her mother and brother that she found me. She'll tell them what I've been doing. If she doesn't betray me again they will. They never liked me much as it was. Especially her mother. Frau Mueller hated me. 'I'm sorry,' I say, stroking her cheek. 'Let me make you a drink and we'll forget about it all for a while.'

She's so trusting that she nods. I despise her for her foolishness where I'm concerned. How can she not realise how dangerous I am to her? How can she be so blind about the things I've had to do to survive in this godforsaken little village? A woman as stupid as that deserves to die.

That's what I tell myself when I slip the needle into the back of her neck. But it doesn't stop me from cradling her in my arms, begging for her forgiveness as she dies. At the last moment she opens her tear-soaked eyes and whispers my name.

'I understand you now,' she says.

What does she mean? What does she understand? Does it mean she forgives me? Does she understand why she could not live? I shake her to try and get her answer, but she is silent.

Did she mean that she finally understands what I am? Did she realise I have always been, even in the days our love was at its strongest?

If she can tell, with her trusting, open nature, then others who are more suspicious will know too.

I cradle her in my arms for hours. Stroking her hair. Crying over her body. I tell her how sorry I am. But it's too late for all that. She's gone from me.

⋆ ⋆ ⋆

Shrewsbury library was quiet when Cara and Guy arrived. Only a few older men and women sat at tables reading books. The librarian pointed them in the direction of the family archives and the old newspapers.

Cara breathed in the smell of old books. There was nothing quite like it in the world. When she was a little girl, a trip to the library once a month had been a treat. Now her stomach knotted a little, because she feared what they might find out about Greta Mueller-Schwartz.

'Where shall we start?' Guy said, opening a drawer full of index cards. There were hundreds in that one drawer alone and it only covered A-Ab. The cabinet had dozens of other drawers.

'I don't know,' said Cara. 'Maybe the electoral register for Midchester in nineteen forty-six? It will give us an idea who was around here at that time.'

'See? I knew there was a reason I needed your help.'

'Actually, I was going to suggest we start at A in the index cards,' Cara said, her eyes sweeping across the cabinet. 'But they go back several generations, so it would take forever just to find people who were around in nineteen-forty-six.'

'I agree. Let's look at the electoral register for that year, then we can try the index cards if we see anyone who could be a possible. You know most of the people in the village. You might be able to tell me about them.'

The electoral registers were in bound volumes on the shelves in the family archives. They also only listed people who were old enough to vote. 'How old would your brother-in-law have been in nineteen forty-six?' she asked Guy.

'Let me think. I was about eight the last time I saw him in nineteen-thirty-eight, and he was in his twenties then. Greta was twenty-eight when they married. He'd be in his early fifties I should think.'

'Good, so we can quickly dispense with women and any men under the age of fifty and over the age of sixty. But let's look from forty-five onwards, just in case we miss him.'

'Good idea. I'm in your hands, Cara.'

Was he flirting with her? She certainly hoped so.

They perused the register for over an hour. Midchester was only a small village but the electoral register also took in several hamlets in the vicinity. There were also a lot of itinerant workers who came in throughout the summer months, lodging with local families or staying in hostel accommodation. It also turned out that most of those listed were done so with an initial and their surname, making it difficult to tell what gender they might be.

As luck would have it, Cara knew a lot of them.

'Abercrombie A, at twenty-nine Station Road is my old headmistress, Mrs

Abercrombie. I think the A stands for Agnes. She'd be about sixty-five now. In fact, yes, she retired about five years ago, so that would be right. She shares her house with another old teacher of mine, Miss Watson, who's a bit younger.'

Cara flicked through another register, which had names beginning with W and found Watson, L.

'I think her name is Lilian. She's still working at the school, though she must be close to retiring. She's supposed to be Mrs Abercrombie's spinster sister, who moved in with her during the war. But they say . . . ' Cara hesitated.

'What?'

'Oh, it's just local gossip, you know. That they're not really sisters. They're . . . erm . . . together.'

'Lesbians, you mean.'

Cara's cheeks burned crimson. She wished she had never started telling him about the two women.

'There's nothing wrong with that. Or at least there shouldn't be. And it's not illegal.'

'Well, no. But you forget Guy, we're in the provinces. Things may well be swinging in London, but around here people are old-fashioned. I reckon they'd still burn witches if they could get away with it. Last year a man and a woman moved into one of the flats above the shops and they weren't married. You should have heard the whispering every time they came into the pub.

'I felt sorry for the girl more than anything because none of the women would talk to her. Nancy and I talked to her because we felt sorry for her. The men were much more forgiving of the bloke. I suppose that's because men tend to be forgiven for such things.'

She was remembering her own transgression and how she had been blamed, while the man's reputation remained intact. 'The couple moved away only a few months later.'

'I suppose I should feel lucky I haven't been hounded out then,' said Guy.

'Well, if you ask me, the sooner you marry Enid, the better,' Cara quipped.

Guy laughed at that. 'Enid is old enough to be my mum. She behaves like a mum to me too. She's the only one who knew the whole truth about me.'

'She's a bit scary, but I'm sure she's a nice woman.'

'She is. She married a German, so she doesn't have the same prejudice as everyone else. He died towards the end of the war and she's never remarried.'

'Oh look,' said Cara, who had been perusing the registers as they talked. 'Here's Peg Bradbourne. She's been living in the Old Constable's house just up the road from Mum's forever. That's what it was, during Victorian times. The constable used to live there.' Cara grimaced. 'Obviously. Then they built the new constable's house, but that name never caught on. They just call it the Police House, which doesn't sound half as romantic, if you ask me. We really should go and speak to Peg about newcomers during or after the war.'

'OK, if you say so.'

'Could your brother-in-law speak English?' Cara asked as they searched more of the register.

'Not that I remember. I only saw him a few times. It was a bit of a surprise when Greta turned up saying she was married.'

'Why?'

'She'd never shown any interest in being anyone's wife. I don't think she'd ever had a boyfriend. Then she met Frederick and it was love at first sight. Or so I'm led to believe.'

'You sound doubtful.'

'It's just that while they were separated, she didn't seem to pine for him in the way most women would when separated from their husbands.'

'Maybe she did in private, but didn't want to upset you or your parents. She must have loved him to come all the way across the world to find him.'

'You're right. It's just my sister was always very expressive in her affections.

My niece suffers from the same problem.'

'Suffers? Is there anything wrong with showing affection?'

'No, not really, even though us Germans are supposed to be very closed and cold in our emotions. We're not really. We have the same passions as everyone else. We just have a different way of showing them. But it makes Brigitte too trusting with people. Then she falls for the wrong man and gets hurt. Greta was too trusting too. When we were in the internment camp, other prisoners would have talked her out of her food if mum and dad hadn't been there to keep an eye on her. She was an angel with a heart as big as the ocean. That's why it's so hard not knowing what happened to her. Who did she trust this time? Was it Frederick? Or did someone else harm her?'

Cara was silent for a while, not knowing what to say next. Guy had become lost in some reverie. She guessed he was thinking about his sister and how she might have come to harm. After giving him a few moments to compose himself, she said gently, 'So you can't think of any reason Frederick would have come to Midchester?'

Guy shook his head and shrugged. 'Not really. From what I know of him, he wasn't a staunch supporter of the Reich, but he knew how to seem to be. It was something a lot of Germans had to do to survive the war. Don't judge them too harshly.'

'No, of course not. People do what they have to do to stay alive and protect their family. That's the same regardless of what nationality they are.'

'Actually, Frederick was the one who got us out of Germany. He made sure we had the right papers. I never asked how he managed it, and I've never had chance to thank him. That's why it's so hard to think he might have hurt Greta. He loved her, of that I am sure. He wanted to see her safe. He even wrote to her for a while, before war broke out properly. Of course, he could never say where he was.'

'Did she have any friends who might have come here? Someone who would know where Frederick went?'

'I don't know. She was a good few years older than me, and I'm sure I was just a pesky little brother to her. Her friends came and went from our house, and some of the girls would make a fuss of me.'

'I bet they did.'

Guy grinned. 'When I was eight years old, I'm pretty certain they only saw me as a younger brother. I didn't mind. I usually got ice-cream out of it. I can't say I ever knew them very well. They were a blur of Leisls and Helgas and Lottes to me. In fact I'm pretty sure there were several Lottes.'

'Would your mother know?'

'Yes, she might. Perhaps I should telephone her and ask. That's something else I never thought of. I knew there was a reason I brought you along.'

'So it wasn't my good looks and

scintillating conversation?' Cara raised a sardonic eyebrow.

'Of course. That goes without saying.'

'I don't mean . . . I mean . . . I don't think I'm good looking. I was just joking.'

'You're not just good looking, Cara, you're utterly gorgeous.'

Their eyes met over the electoral registers. It was not the most romantic of settings, but Cara still felt her heart swell.

'We should get on,' she whispered, hardly able to talk.

About ten minutes later, Cara was still going through the B's, checking and re-checking, trying to think who was who. It did not help that some families gave their sons the same name as the father and grandfather, all of whom were still living, so there were lots of R Barretts or W Browns.

She kept coming back to one name: Black, E. She had a vague recollection of German lessons at school.

'Guy, what did you say your sister's

married name was?'

'Schwartz.'

'Doesn't that mean black in English?'

'Yes, it does.'

'Frederick Schwartz?'

'That's right. Why? What have you found?'

Cara turned the book towards him and showed him the register. 'Eric Black. The man we're having dinner with tonight. It might be a long shot, but Schwartz would obviously be Black, but he might also have used the 'Eric' part of his first name.'

'My God, you're a genius! Maybe this is what Anderson found?' Guy said excitedly.

Before leaving for Shrewsbury, Cara had called back to her mother's and borrowed a notebook. She wrote down the details. 'Do you think that if he was Frederick, you'd recognise him?'

'I'm not sure after all this time,' said Guy. 'But it's worth a try. He must know who I am by now.'

'Yes, news travels fast in Midchester.

Perhaps that's why he invited you, to see if you do know him. Oh, you must be careful, Guy.' She put her hand over his. 'If he . . . '

She did not want to say anymore. Not for the first time in the past few days an icy finger trailed down her spine. Something bad happening to Guy was too awful to contemplate.

'You're thinking that if he killed Greta, then he might kill me to stop his identity being known.'

Cara nodded, frowning. 'Who knows what he's capable of? We should look in the newspaper too, and see what he was up to around that time. I'm sure he owned it then, and he has a habit of filling the pages with his own exploits. The other candidates in the mayoral elections have called him on his overt self-aggrandisement several times, but he never stops. I'm convinced the paper is something of a vanity project for him. We should also speak to Peg. She'll know all about him, I'm sure. If you feel you want to trust her, that is.'

'Do you trust Peg?'

'Oh, yes. With my life.'

'Then I trust her too.'

'Would your brother-in-law have spied for Hitler?'

'I guess he would have, if it meant staying alive. But like I say, I don't even know if he spoke English. He'd have to be bloody good at it to infiltrate a typical British village like Midchester. From what I remember of him, he was always very correct and rather dull. I can't see him having the imagination to be a spy. But again, who knows what he did to survive?'

'It's something else to ask your mother. She might know.'

'Why would he want to spy here?' Guy asked. 'It seems rather a quiet backwater.'

'There was an American airbase nearby during the war, but now it only has private planes for chartered flights.'

'Ah, yes, I passed that on the way to Midchester. I guess that's his motive for being here then. He must have decided to stay on after the war. Having a German wife would not have gone down well with the locals. He'd have had a job explaining her and a seven year-old daughter.'

'Yes, he would,' said Cara, sadly. 'They're not bad people in Midchester. They work hard all their lives and they're honest, for the most part. They're just a bit limited in their world view.'

They spent another half an hour looking through the electoral registers, but despite Cara knowing a lot of the people listed in them, there was no-one who stood out as being a possible Frederick Schwartz.

'Let's look through some of the newspapers, and then we'll have to get back,' said Guy. 'All I can think about now is meeting Eric Black.'

'Yes, me too,' Cara agreed.

They scrolled through the microfiche records and found the papers for nineteen-forty-six. They had reached

December when they found it in the local paper.

Fifth Columnist Hanged

An unknown woman was hanged as a German spy yesterday. The woman was arrested after being seen around the Shropshire area, close to the American airbase. She was thought to be in her mid-thirties, five feet six inches tall, with blonde hair. Anyone having any information about the woman's identity should inform the police.

Cara looked up at Guy and saw the colour drain from his face.

'Is that her?' Cara asked.

'It sounds like her . . . ' Guy seemed barely able to speak.

'Oh Guy,' she whispered, taking his hand. 'I'm so sorry.'

8

1946

I can barely bring myself to do what needs to be done. But if I'm to get her up to the bonfire, it's the only way. If I'm stopped, I can always say it's my contribution to the festivities and pray that my ruse works better than the one young Sammy and his friends tried.

It feels like a violation, removing her clothes and replacing them with the clothes of his tramp mother. I'll have to get rid of her clothes in some other way, just in case they don't burn through properly. Someone might have remembered her and what she was wearing.

'I'm sorry, my love,' I murmur, as I begin preparing her for the bonfire. 'If there were any other way, we could have lived happily together. Even with Brigitte.' I explain to her how much I like my life here. How good it feels to be a big fish in a small pond. One day I'll be an even bigger fish. Then I can guide this country towards being what it should be. She stares back at me blankly, accusingly, so that I have to close her eyes.

Soon she is ready. She looks grotesque with the paper bag over her head. It was not enough that I killed her. I have violated her too. Made her into something inhuman. What's more, I have to keep her here until it gets dark.

When I can no longer bear looking at her, I put her into the boot of the car. I sit and wait for dusk to fall. I can't risk being seen, so I drive the car up through the trees, at the back of the common. There's an old footpath there that no one ever uses. It leads up to the Roman ruins.

My guess is that none of the locals has walked that route since that old Jew finished his digging, and the area was plundered by other archaeologists for artefacts. Occasionally, in summer, day trippers hike the lanes in the area, but it's November, so there's no risk of that.

She's so slight, like a wisp of air, that I lift her easily in and out of the boot. I carry her to the bonfire and lean her against the side, while I walk around, looking for a large enough gap in which to put her. Anyone glancing up from the village at this time of the evening will think that it's just another Guy Fawkes put here by the children.

Someone is coming! I wait behind the bonfire, holding my breath. Damn! It's that dirty little gypsy girl. What's her name? Cara, that's it. Why does this country allow such people to live? It's an abomination.

She's seen the body and is walking towards it. If I have to kill her, and shove her into the bonfire, I will. No-one will miss her, except that vile gypsy mother of hers and no-one cares about her feelings. I've heard the women talking about her behind her back. They'd probably thank me for giving her a reason to leave Midchester. They don't much like people who are different here and Martha Potter is very different, with her chaotic house and feral children.

I'm just about to reach out and grab the kid when she starts running away. She's realised that the effigy is real. She'll send others up here and then what shall I do?

I'm close to panicking, and it seems like minutes pass when really it's only moments. Then I see Sammy watching me from the lane. He's standing near to my car, smoking a cigarette. Good. It's time he learned just how deep a hole he has dug for himself by helping me.

'Sammy.' I keep my tone mild, welcoming. 'Come here for a minute, will you?'

* * *

1966

Cara let herself in through the back door of The Quiet Woman. Her stomach churned at the thought of facing Nancy, but it had to be done. She needed a dress for the dinner party, and all her clothes were in her room at the pub.

Guy had gone home to get changed and they had agreed to meet in the village square before walking to Eric Black's house.

She crept up the stairs, thinking that Nancy might be in the bar, serving the lunch time crowd. So it gave her a fright when Nancy's bedroom door opened. Nancy emerged, tying up her dressing gown. 'Oh, it's you, Cara.'

'Yes. Sorry. I need my clothes.'

'Well, you know where they are.'

Cara's heart dropped. Nancy's mood had not improved since the morning. 'I do. Erm . . . haven't you opened the pub today, Nancy? It's nearly two o'clock.'

'I've had other things on. It won't hurt them to go one session without drink.'

'I suppose not.' Cara did not know

what else to say.

This was not like Nancy at all. She always worked hard, and as far as Cara remembered, had never missed an opening time. Even when she was ill, she insisted on making sure the customers were served.

Before going into her room, Cara looked back at Nancy and said, 'Whatever has happened between us, I hope you still realise that I'm still your friend. If there's anything I can do.'

'Thank you, Cara, but I really think it's time you moved on.'

Feeling as if Nancy had plunged a dagger in her heart, Cara almost staggered. 'OK, if that's what you think.' She swallowed back a lump in her throat that threatened to choke her.

'No, I mean it. You always were too good for this place, and I've held you back. It's time you followed your dream. I realised that last night when I saw you enjoying yourself so much with Guy Sullivan. This will never be that sort of pub, Cara, but I can see why you'd be attracted to that type of life, of champagne cocktails and gorgeous men.'

'I've never thought I was too good for the pub, Nancy.'

'No, pet, I know you haven't.' Nancy voice softened. 'But you do need to do something more with your life than be a barmaid. You don't want to end up like me.'

'I'd be very proud to be like you.'

'No, you wouldn't, pet. You only say that because you don't really know me. Come here.' Nancy held out her arms, and Cara accepted her hug.

'Why are you saying this?' Cara started to cry, feeling as if she was saying a permanent goodbye to her friend.

It felt like the end of an era, but there was something more. Nancy was not just saying goodbye. It seemed as though she was severing all ties, not just with Cara but with the world.

'If it's about last night, I can't say I'm any sorrier than I am.'

'There's nothing to apologise for, Cara. I over-reacted. But I can't have you living here right now, so it's best you go. I'm sure you'll find another job.'

'Actually,' said Cara, 'I've already got one.'

'That was quick.' Nancy seemed a bit put out. Had she hoped Cara would struggle without her as a friend and mentor?

'I'm helping Guy to find his sister. He's paying me.'

For some reason, Nancy backed away, as if she had been given an electric shock. 'I see. What brought that on?'

'Well, he wants to know what happened to her. Actually, we think we do now. There was a piece in the local paper about an unnamed woman being hanged as a German spy in nineteen forty-six. It matches her description.'

'Well, there won't be much more work for you to do then.'

'He still wants to know why she came to Midchester.'

'If they think she was spying . . . '

Cara shook her head vehemently. 'No, she wasn't a spy. She didn't even like the Nazis. She's from a good family who managed to get away from Germany when they realised the way things were going.'

'When you think about it, Cara, that's a good cover story.'

'What are you saying, Nancy? That you think Guy is lying?' Cara felt her temper flare.

'No, I'm only saying that he might not know everything about his big sister.'

'Well perhaps he didn't, but he knows she wasn't a spy. She spent most of the war in an internment camp, with him and his parents, and her little girl. There aren't many opportunities to spy when you're in those conditions.'

'Alright, Cara, calm down.' Nancy raised a hand in supplication. 'I'm only saying that there may be other things Guy might not want to find out.'

'Why? What do you know?'

'Me? I don't know anything. I'm just speculating, pet.'

Cara wanted to believe her, but she could not help suspecting that Nancy knew more than she was saying.

She would have been a teenager when Greta came to Midchester in nineteen-forty-six. Had she seen her and was keeping it quiet for some reason?

'I'd better get my things then,' said Cara, feeling somewhat deflated. She had hoped that things would be put right with Nancy, but their relationship was even more strained than it had been when she left in a huff that morning.

Going into her room, Cara threw some clothes into a suitcase. She couldn't carry everything, so it would mean having to come back.

She wondered if she should hand her keys back to Nancy. She had no right to them anymore.

When her suitcase was packed, she went out and crossed the landing to

Nancy's bedroom. She was just about to knock when she thought she heard voices. One of them was a man's.

Tiptoeing down the stairs, Cara left the pub for what was to be the very last time.

* * *

Guy was finding it hard to remember why he was at Eric Black's dinner party. Cara sat opposite him at the table, dressed in a silver crocheted A-line dress. She had teased her light brown hair into a beehive, and put black kohl around her eyes, accentuating the blue.

He wondered if she knew just how stunning she was. At that moment, he felt she could grace the cover of any magazine, giving Twiggy and Jean Shrimpton a run for their money. He would quite happily spend the rest of his life just looking at her. No, not just looking at her. Talking to her too. She was funny and clever, with no idea of the affect she was having on him or any man.

But for some reason she looked pensive tonight. She had been fine when they arrived, until she was introduced to the other guests. One particular guest in fact. A man called Tony Weston, who had come with his wife, a pale, plump woman called Sandra. Sandra Weston kept giving Cara waspish looks.

Guy wondered what the story was there, other than that Tony could not take his eyes off Cara. But as Weston was not the only man there to be stunned by her beauty, Guy could hardly blame him for that.

Weston was in his thirties, with a beer gut and hair full of dandruff. He was getting the red nose that typified a heavy drinker. There were signs that he had been a good-looking man at one time in his life, but those looks were quickly fading.

Guy managed to drag his own eyes away from Cara and peruse the rest of the people assembled. There were several local councillors and their wives. Guy had been introduced to them and had promptly forgotten all their names.

He turned his attention to their host. Whether Eric Black was Frederick Schwartz or not, Guy could not tell. There was nothing about him that he recognised, but that might have had a lot to do with Black's attire. Despite it being a formal dinner party, with every other man dressed in a smart suit, Black was dressed in jeans and a tie-dyed shirt. His hair, or what was left of it, was shoulder length. His side-burns ran down to his chin, spreading out like black and grey mould. He wore several strings of beads around his neck. The look would have suited a man thirty years younger, but on a man in his fifties who wanted to make his name in politics, it looked inappropriate.

The house, an art deco building, had been decorated in the latest fashion, with lots of black and chrome, and plastic chairs that one stuck to when bare-legged. Sheepskin rugs hung on the walls, while abstract sculptures were dotted around the floor. The paintings were mainly Andy Warhol, alongside photographs by David Bailey.

'Of course,' Black was saying to one of the other guests, 'until you visit India and drink in the spirituality, you are not a whole person. The things Barbara and I saw over there . . . ' At that he glanced at the woman at the other end of the table.

Barbara Price had been introduced as Black's assistant, but there was clearly more than that to their relationship. Guy remembered the tale Cara had told about the couple 'living in sin' above the shop who had been hounded out of Midchester. He wondered if that would have been the case if the young couple had been as rich as Eric Black. In Guys' experience, the wealthy could ignore any number of social mores and would never be ostracised.

Mr Black and Miss Price were lovers, of that Guy was convinced. Miss Price was as striking as her lover, albeit in a different way. She was of statuesque build and almost a head taller than Black, with a slender but muscular body. She wore a powder blue kaftan, which was decorated with a sequined peacock applique. Her hair was cut in an asymmetric style, with half a heavily lacquered fringe covering one eye. Despite being around Black's age, she carried the latest fashions off with more aplomb than he did.

'Have you ever been to India, Mr Sullivan?' she asked, caressing her wine glass with long fingers.

'Yes, I visited a few years ago.'

'What were your impressions of it?'

'I thought it had an awful lot of very hungry people and that the only ones making money were those who spouted quasi-spiritual crap to gullible Western travellers.'

Someone choked on their drink, and there were a few gasps. No-one said anything. Guy had realised early in his career that a famous actor could get away with saying just about anything.

Guy realised he was being a bit harsh, and that it was unfair to use his fame as an excuse to misbehave, but something about the dinner party irked him. Black was clearly a big fake, but someone else in the room was too. They were just better at hiding it. Something dark and malevolent hung in the air, yet he could not trace its source.

'I hear the Beatles are going over there,' said one of the other ladies. 'They're getting a little pretentious if you ask me.'

'I agree,' said Guy. 'It's Mrs Abercrombie, isn't it?' He remembered her because they had only just been talking about her and her supposed sister, Miss Watson, that afternoon.

'Yes, that's right, but do call me Agnes. And this is my sister, Lilian.' Guy immediately warmed to Agnes. She had a full, matronly body and bright, intelligent eyes. Lilian Watson was the polar opposite. She was bird-like and fragile looking. There was no possible way they could be sisters.

'Cara told me you were her headmistress. Tell me; was she very naughty at school?' He winked at Cara who was looking at him with mock horror. But it seemed to relax her. She gave him a dazzling smile.

'I'll have you know I was a good girl.'

'She was a good girl,' said Lilian Watson, primly. 'At least she was when she was in my class.'

'Unlike her brother, Freddie,' said Mrs Abercrombie. 'But he turned out all right in the end. Ended up at Oxford, didn't he?'

'Yes, that's right. He still teaches there.'

'I remember Freddie,' said Barbara Price. 'He is a handsome boy. Has he ever married?'

'No . . . erm . . . no, he never married,' said Cara. 'He lives with his friend, Ralph. I mean, they share a house.' Her voice faded at the end of the sentence.

She looked from Mrs Abercrombie to

Miss Watson as though mentioning her brother and his friend had brought them to mind. Guy wanted to put his arms around her and tell her it didn't matter that Freddie wanted to live with Ralph.

'Renting is so expensive,' said Mrs Abercrombie, kindly. 'That's why my sister and I share.'

Cara nodded. 'And it's even more expensive in Oxford.'

'So,' said one of the other men at the table. 'You don't think there's anything new to learn about spirituality from visiting India, Mr Sullivan?'

He had been introduced to Guy as Reverend Andrew Cunningham. He was a strikingly handsome man in his forties, and what one might call 'trendy' for a vicar. He was accompanied by his wife, Meredith, whom Guy had already met briefly on the night they found Carl Anderson dead. She was as beautiful as her husband was handsome and they seemed to make the perfect couple.

'I'm not against travelling to broaden the mind, Reverend. I just don't think the answer to the meaning of life can be found at the bottom of a hashish pipe.'

The reverend grinned. 'No, I absolutely agree. I used to work in the East End of London, before I got this cushy gig. I found that drugs cause more problems than they solve.'

'Of course, I'm anti-drugs,' said Eric Black. 'But I still think we've much to learn from the East. I met a man who gave me the perfect diet to counter my diabetes, but my own doctor is too set in his ways and won't allow me to follow it.'

'You're diabetic?' Guy frowned, struggling to remember if he ever knew that about Frederick Schwartz. 'How long have you had diabetes?'

'I've been insulin dependent all my life. Unfortunately it meant I couldn't join in with the war effort, though I did my best in the Home Guard.'

'In Midchester?'

'No, not Midchester. I was born and

raised in Newcastle. I didn't come here until . . . oh when was it? The end of Forty-five, I think. The war hadn't officially ended by then, but it was all over bar the shouting as they say. That's when I met Barbara, and we began the newspaper together.'

'That reminds me, Mr Black,' Cara said. 'We were looking at old newspapers in the library today.' Guy and Cara had discussed before arriving that they would be honest about what they were doing, to see if there was any reaction.

'Yes,' Guy said, 'I'm trying to find my sister, Greta.'

'Oh yes, I had heard,' said Black.

Guy searched his eyes for some sign of guilt, or even recognition, but either Black was a very good actor, or there was nothing to see.

'We found an article in the paper,' said Cara. 'It was your paper. About an unnamed German woman who had been hanged as a spy. It appeared around December, nineteen-forty-six. Do you remember it?'

Black was silent for a while, then said, 'Not really. We publish hundreds of stories every year, as you know, Cara. Which reminds me, I'm still waiting for your expose on Mr Sullivan.'

Everyone laughed at that, but Cara looked stricken. She glanced at Guy, horrified. 'It wasn't an expose,' she said.

'I know that,' Guy said, smiling back at her.

'I'm just teasing,' said Black. Was he, thought Guy. Or was he just playing for time? 'Actually I think I was away that month. Can you remember, Barbara?'

'It was a long time ago. I'm not sure you were, Eric.'

'Oh yes, I definitely was,' said Black, emphatically. 'You must remember.'

'Do you remember the story, Miss Price?' asked Guy.

'I told you, it's Barbara,' she said with a provocative smile. 'Let me think. No, I don't remember it, but let me have a look at our own copies and maybe when I see the wording it will ring a bell. We have lots of freelance journalists, like Cara here, so it might have been written by one of them. Sometimes we just get stuff in from news agencies, and we cover it without paying too much attention. Was there a by-line?' The by-line was the name of the reporter who had written the story.

Cara shook her head. 'No. I checked.'

'That's odd. Normally it would say who'd written it, or where it had come from. Mind you, if Eric was away then, I might have brought in a temporary editor. I tend to get rushed off my feet.'

'Do you remember who that was?' asked Guy.

'Oh, now let me see. No, no, I can't remember. As I say, it all depends if Eric was away or not. But, I'll find out for you. I'm sure you want to get to the bottom of this, Guy.'

'Yes, I do. My sister was no spy.'

'Oh, I'm sure she wasn't.' Barbara's patronising tone annoyed him. It suggested she believed every word of it. 'I'm sure it was a dreadful mistake on the part of the authorities.'

'It must have been hard for you, not knowing where she was all this time?' Meredith Cunningham said, in sympathetic tones. At least she didn't patronise him. 'And then to read that . . . '

Guy nodded in agreement. 'Yes, it's been hard, especially for my niece, Brigitte.'

'I don't know if this helps,' said Reverend Cunningham, 'but they would keep records and maybe even belongings at the prison where your sister was kept. Perhaps you could find out more that way. If they have personal affects, you might be able to identify them as hers. At least then you'll know for certain.'

'Yes, thank you, Reverend. But there was no mention of where she was imprisoned. In fact, I get the impression that it was all done very quickly and with little ceremony.'

'It will be on record somewhere. The court files will certainly be available, unless they're locked under the Official

Secrets Act. London is the place to go, I should think. I've got an old friend who works in intelligence. Maybe he can help you. I could give him a ring if you like.'

'That's very kind of you, Reverend. I'd like to try that, if it's no problem. What do you say to a trip down to London, Cara?'

'If you want me to come with you.'

'Of course. You have all the best ideas.'

'Well, that's all settled then,' said Eric Black. He looked down at his food and frowned.

9

1946

I have to navigate the lane without lights, just in case those running up to the bonfire see me through the trees. Sammy sits in the passenger seat, trembling.

'I wouldn't have done it if I'd known,' he whimpered, more like a ten year old than a teenager. 'Who is she?'

'She's a bad person who was going to do bad things to Midchester,' I lie. 'Would you believe she's a bloody Jerry? They'd have hanged her anyway. I just saved them the job. We all have to do what we can to stop another war.' Or to start one. 'Don't think of it as breaking the law, Sammy. Think of it as defending your country, just like you said you wanted to.'

'I don't know. It feels wrong somehow.' He looked at me sideways, his voice tremulous. 'You're a strange one. Nobody knows you around here, yet you turn up and start running things. How do I know I can trust you, that you won't kill me too?'

It seems he's brighter than I thought.

'Because we're British, Sammy. We're in this together. Just help me bury the body then you can go about your life and I'll go about mine. Only we'll know how brave we've been, but that doesn't matter, does it?'

I'm trying to appeal to his sense of the dramatic. He'll be able to pretend to himself that he's the hero of all this. But he doesn't really have the gumption for heroics. I'm going to have to force him.

I have to think on my feet, so I quickly find the spot where she won't be disturbed. At least not for a very long time. I see all the records of the planning committee and there are no digs planned in the near future.

As luck would have it, there's a shovel in the boot, just in case of bad weather. Around here, when winter comes, people can be snowed in for weeks. There's a torch in the glove box too. I tell him to get that.

'Dig the grave and there's a tenner in it for you,' I say.

'I want more than a tenner to hide a dead body. And I want proper money, too. That fiver you gave me was dodgy. That's why I came looking for you. But I never expected to find any of this though.'

'OK, twenty pounds. But don't forget, Sammy, she's wearing your mother's clothes and she's dressed up in the way you and your friends did when you tried to fool the judges at the Guy Fawkes competition. You're implicated in this more than I am.'

I see the words striking home. 'No,' he whispers.

'Oh yes, Sammy. You're in this up to your neck. Which is a very appropriate phrase, because if they find out about her, they'll hang you.'

'They'll hang you too. Anyway, I thought you said we were doing something good. Why would they hang us for that?'

I swear under my breath. Now he decides to be intelligent!

'We won't be able to prove what she was. She can hardly tell them, can she?'

It takes a while and my temper is reaching tipping point, but eventually he starts to dig. But he's pathetic at it. The ground is hard, and he barely makes a dent. The boy hasn't done a day's work in his life.

'Oh, give it to me!'

I snatch the shovel from him, and dig. Nearly an hour later, with the muscles on my arms burning, the ground is deep enough to bury two people, let alone one. We haul her in.

'You start pushing the earth back in with your hands, and I'll use the shovel,' I command.

Sammy kneels down, just as I hoped

he would. I raise the shovel and aim for his skull . . .

* * *

1966

'You look stunning.' Tony leered over Cara while she was looking up at one of the portraits. The guests had moved to a different room to drink coffee.

'Go away,' she hissed. Of all the people to turn up at Black's party, why did it have to be Tony? Cara almost wilted under the hateful looks of his wife when they were introduced. Tony must have told her about Cara. He probably took some sick pleasure in confessing.

'You're certainly moving up in the world, Cara, hobnobbing with famous actors.'

'I don't want to talk to you, Tony. Go away.'

'Why? Doesn't your friend know about me?'

Cara shivered. No, Guy did not know about him and she had no idea what he would think if he did know. She had not exactly covered herself in glory where Tony was concerned.

'I think your wife wants you,' she said, pointedly.

'I'm running a club in Hereford now. All the best people go there. We might even get The Who to do a gig. When Mr Famous Actor gets tired of you, you can come and dance for me there. You know, like you used to when we were alone.'

She turned on him, her face aflame, and was horrified to see Guy standing nearby, listening to every word.

'She's right,' said Guy, stony-faced. 'Your wife is looking for you.' He was head and shoulders taller than Tony, so easily dominated him.

'Are you OK?' he asked Cara, when Tony had slunk away to find Sandra.

'Yes, I'm fine.'

'Do you want to tell me about that?'

'No. I mean, not here.'

'OK, we'll talk about it later, on the way home.'

And later you won't want to know me anymore, she thought miserably. She went to sit on the sofa, next to Mrs Abercrombie.

She could not wait to get away from this awful dinner party. Guy had been uncharacteristically rude about Black's visit to India, and yet she understood why. There was a sensation of evil under all the polite talk that threatened to infect everyone; no-one seemed to be enjoying themselves. She had seen the reverend and Meredith looking at the clock several times, muttering something about getting back for the babysitter.

Cara felt unwelcome in Black's house without an explicit reason for feeling that way. No-one had said anything unkind to her, but there was a definite undercurrent. It might have been because Tony Weston was there, but she didn't think so. The emotion of revulsion he invoked in her was different to the unease that caused her tummy to tie up in a tight knot. She shivered, feeling that someone had just walked over her grave.

Trying to catch Guy's eye, she wanted to tell him it was time to leave, but he was not looking her way — although he, too, seemed ill at ease.

'You'll never guess who I saw the other day,' Mrs Abercrombie was saying to no-one in particular.

'Who?' asked the Reverend.

'Young Sammy . . . oh what was his surname? He was hardly ever at school. You know who I mean, Lilian. His mother was an alcoholic, and one day he just upped and disappeared. I saw him hanging around near the milestone just outside Midchester. I didn't recognise him at first. He's got all that long greasy hair that young men have nowadays.'

Mrs Abercrombie looked at Eric Black, with his long locks, and bit her lip. 'Well, it's not so bad when they wash it. But then he turned towards me and I realised who he was.'

'I don't think I remember him,' said Eric Black.

'Oh you do, Eric,' said Miss Watson. 'He used to hang around up here all the time.'

'That's news to me,' said Barbara Price. 'Is there something you haven't told me Eric?'

Everyone laughed at that. Except for Eric Black.

'Well, not all the time,' said Miss Watson, getting flustered. 'What I mean is I saw him coming from here a few times. Actually it might have only been once or twice. He used to run around with young Nancy from the pub.'

'Yes, that's what I was going to say next,' said Mrs Abercrombie. 'I went a bit further up the road and saw Nancy. She was driving towards the milestone. I saw her stop there in my rear view mirror, then Sammy got in and they drove off.'

'Oh that's a funny thing,' said Tony. 'We passed the pub on the way here and it was shut.'

'Nancy's not very well,' Cara said, believing she should defend her friend. Mrs Abercrombie's revelation had given her an idea who the man was in Nancy's room earlier that day and why she had been told to leave. Why would Nancy not tell her the truth? They normally shared everything and Cara would not have disapproved of Nancy having a man stay over.

More importantly, what reason had Sammy Granger got to hide away from everyone?

'So you're not working there any-more, Cara,' said Black.

'No. We both felt it was time I moved on.'

'Perhaps we can find you a perma-nent place on the paper.'

'That would be wonderful. I mean, I'm helping Guy at the moment, to find his sister, but if there's anything permanent, I'd be really grateful.'

Despite being grateful, Cara was confused. Eric Black had not much liked her first article, though he had been kinder about those that followed. Yet here he was offering her a full-time job. She decided not to look a gift horse in the mouth. Guy would not be around forever and she had to have some form of employment.

'You'd have to be an apprentice of sorts, so the pay wouldn't be very much, but we'll find a place for you, won't we, Barbara?'

'Yes, there's always room for good writers on the Chronicle.'

'Don't steal her away from me too soon,' said Guy. 'I might have further plans for her yet.'

'I bet you do,' said Tony, lasciviously. Cara resisted the urge to slap him.

She could not wait for the dinner party to be over. Meeting him again had been excruciating, and seeing his paunchy belly and dandruff speckled hair, she began to wonder what she had ever seen in him. There was a time when he had seemed to be all that was glamorous in a man. Seeing him in the same room as Guy, she realised just how ordinary he was. What an idiot she had been!

The dinner party ended around ten-thirty and people began to drift away. The Reverend and Mrs Cunningham offered Cara and Guy a lift, but Guy politely refused.

'We'll enjoy the walk,' he said. Cara guessed that what he really wanted to do was talk to her about the night and, worse still, about Tony.

'I see. Oh well, I suppose you've got your love to keep you warm,' said the Reverend. It was said lightly and without the same inference as Tony's earlier comment. Still Cara blushed.

'Cara,' said Guy as they walked down the lane towards Midchester, 'I don't want to dampen your enthusiasm, but don't you think it's odd that Black is offering you a full-time job, just as we show up telling him everything about my sister?'

'Don't you think I'm capable of being a reporter?' Cara was feeling tetchy, partly because of the atmosphere at the dinner party and partly due to seeing Tony again. Guy's question riled her even further.

'I think you're capable of being anything you want to be. I just don't want you to be hurt, that's all. Talking of which, do you want to tell me about Tony?'

'Not really.'

They stepped aside as several cars passed them, carrying the other diners home. Cara began to wish they'd taken up the Reverend's offer. She would not be having this awkward conversation with Guy for a start.

'I'm surprised you don't already know, with the way people gossip in Midchester.'

'They're too busy gossiping about me being German at the moment. Tomorrow they'll be gossiping about my sister being hanged as a spy. What did you do that was so shocking?'

'I had an affair with a married man.'

'Oh.'

'This is going to sound like an excuse, but it isn't. I didn't know he was married, and then when I found out, I even considered ignoring the fact.'

The confession had been dragged from the depths of Cara's soul. She sighed and a wisp of air rose from her mouth into the cold night air.

'Tony was a buyer for the brewery. He used to visit the pub and flirt with us both. I thought he was glamorous at the time. He was a lot smarter back then, and better looking. I can't believe how he's let himself go. Besides, I hadn't had that much male attention.'

'I find that hard to believe.'

'In case you haven't noticed, the majority of men in Midchester are over fifty years of age. Either that or they're under twenty years of age. Only the vicar is reasonably young and he's completely smitten with his wife.'

'I can see why. She's a firecracker.'

'Yes, she's lovely.' Cara suppressed a pang of jealousy. Not that she blamed

Guy for being impressed with Meredith Cunningham. 'Anyway, I started going out with Tony.' She paused. 'It became serious . . . you know . . . '

She hoped she would not have to be more explicit. The conversation was excruciating enough as it was.

'I found out about Sandra when we got a call at the pub one day asking if Tony had arrived yet. Sandra had gone into labour and naturally wanted him to be with her. I was devastated, but the following week he telephoned and told me about how they hadn't made love for ages, and that he was sure the baby wasn't his. He told me lots of other things about how unhappy she made him. I was very nearly fooled. I wanted to believe that I could make him happy where she couldn't. A few days later, we had another phone call at the pub. Not his wife this time, but some other girl he had over in Hereford, wondering if we'd seen him. I ended it then, even when he turned up at the pub with protestations of love and more lies.'

She shivered and pulled her thick woollen coat around her, wishing she had not worn such a skimpy dress.

'So that's me. Marriage wrecker extraordinaire.'

'I think you're being too hard on yourself, Cara. You're allowed to make mistakes.'

'It's just that when I look back and realise how gullible I was, I hate myself for it. Then when I saw him tonight . . . '

'Do you still love him?' It sounded as though the answer mattered to Guy.

'God no. I don't know why I ever did. Mind you, he wasn't that paunchy back then. He didn't drink so much either. Did you see the way he was knocking them back tonight? Even so, he's a creep and always has been. I don't know why I didn't see it.'

'Love is blind, according to the cliché.'

'Do you think that's really true? Do you think that you can love someone and completely fail to see how awful they are?'

'Women have married murderers and rapists before now, and when their husbands are caught, they still don't believe that he is capable of such violence. I gather that psychopaths are very good at hiding what they are to others.'

'Oh, so only women are gullible. Is that what you're saying?'

Guy laughed. 'No, men can be stupid when it comes to love.'

'Were you stupid? With Selina Cartier, I mean.'

Guy stiffened. 'That's a different story altogether,' he said, abruptly. 'It's nothing like yours.'

'Oh, I'm sorry, Guy,' said Cara, annoyed that he turned out to have the same double standards as everyone else. 'I thought we were sharing here, but obviously I got it wrong. Of course your affair will be forgivable because you're a man!'

She stormed on ahead, nearly falling into a pothole on the road. Guy caught her just before she fell, holding her firmly by the shoulders. She felt safe in his arms, but wondered if it was only an illusion. The way he looked at her suggested a hidden danger. Not violent or malevolent, but dangerous all the same. She could easily forget all the reasons he might not be right for her and just offer herself up to him. It pained her to realise that she had probably learned nothing from her experience with Tony.

'Just trust me, Cara. I'm not like Tony Weston.'

'Aren't you?'

'No. For a start, I'd never want you to dance for anyone else but me.' There was something about the way he said the word 'dance' that gave it a more intimate meaning.

The mood changed. It held a different sort of intensity, one that bound them together. He lowered his head and his lips found hers. She returned his kiss, feverishly. It had been so long since she had let a man this close to her. Oddly, it felt like the first time she had ever been kissed. Certainly no-one had made her feel the way Guy did, as he enclosed her in his arms, deepening the kiss. Oh yes, she thought, I'm definitely lost.

She was vaguely aware of a car passing them on the road, but they were too wrapped up in each other to take much notice. She coiled her fingers in his hair and moaned as the passion between them rose. She pulled away reluctantly, determined to show some restraint, even if it killed her to do so.

'Guy, I don't want to rush anything.'

'I understand, darling,' he replied. 'We have all the time in the world.'

Did they? Cara wondered about that as they walked back to Midchester, holding hands. Perhaps she should just make the most of him while he was there, because soon he would return to Hollywood, where actresses more beautiful than she could ever hope to be would make him quickly forget her.

They discussed the evening and Guy's impressions of everyone he had met, especially Black.

'He's a fake,' said Guy. 'But whether he's the fake we're looking for is another matter.'

'It was strange, wasn't it?' said Cara, huddling into him. 'The atmosphere I mean. Everyone seemed so nice, and yet . . . '

'There was definitely something malevolent in the air.'

'I don't think people could wait to get away. I was glad to get away and thought it was because of Tony. It lingered too. I don't think I felt better until . . . ' She placed her cheek against his upper arm.

'The kiss,' he whispered, kissing her on the top of her head.

'Mmm, the kiss.'

They fell into blissful silence.

After a few minutes, Cara murmured, 'Guy?'

'No. You're right. We should wait.'

'Oh.'

'It isn't that I don't want you. Far from it. You have no idea how much thought I have to give to my taxes right now just so I don't disgrace myself in the open air. But I don't think you quite trust me yet, and taking you to bed too soon isn't going to make you feel any better.'

'Oh, I don't know about that.'

He laughed softly. 'I'm sure it will make us both feel very good. But then you'll wake up in the morning and wonder if I've used you. I don't want you to feel that way.'

'Maybe I'll have used you,' she said, impishly.

'In which case, I'd wake up with a big smile on my face.'

Cara giggled. 'Would you? I'd like to see that.'

'Streuth, woman, what are you trying to do to me? Here I am, trying to behave like a gentleman and you're trying to corrupt me.'

'I don't think you'll need my help with that. I read the gossip columns. I know what Hollywood is like.'

Guy became more serious. 'It's

certainly hard to keep your morals over there.'

'You sound as if you hate it.'

'I don't hate it. It's been good to me. I just dislike the way actors are treated like gods. Eventually they come to believe it, and think they can get away with anything. Sometimes they're right. They can. Like me tonight at the dinner party. I was really rude to our host, yet no-one chastised me. A thing like that can make a man forget how to behave.'

'So why do you stay in Hollywood?'

'I need to earn the money to do what I really want to do.'

'What's that?'

'I want to make films in Australia. There's a lot of talent over there that doesn't have an outlet and there are a lot of stories that never get told. I'd love to set up my own film studio in Sidney. If this next film does well, that's what I intend to do. Hollywood won't see me for dust.'

'That sounds exciting.'

'Yeah, I think so too. Maybe you

could help me. Would you like to go to Australia?'

Cara did not know how to answer that. Was he asking her to go with him as a lover or just as an employee?

'I think it would be exciting to be part of something new,' was all she could say. 'But I don't know a thing about films.'

'They need writers and researchers just like any other medium. You're good at that.'

'You've no idea if I'm good or not. You've never read anything of mine.'

She feared that he was stringing her along, just as Tony had. He could just be trying to fill her head with dreams about being be a star, or if not a star, then a big player behind the scenes.

'I can tell you're good.'

'Oh, you can, can you? Well, perhaps you should tell that to all those publishers who've turned down my stories.'

'I will. Just give me their names and addresses.'

Cara laughed. 'You're mad,' she said.

Guy was about to reply, then he stopped, open-mouthed, looking into the distance. They were on the outskirts of the village, near to the railway station.

'There's a fire,' he said.

Cara turned and looked towards the village centre and saw flames rising into the air. She screamed and began to run.

10

So Sammy Granger is back! Damn, I should have killed that boy when I had the chance. Who would have thought he would be so quick to run when I held the shovel over his head? I thought I'd at least chased him off for good. Where will he be? There's only one place if Nancy was picking him up at the milestone. What if he isn't there? It's a chance I'll have to take.

How to get rid of him for good? That's the problem. I don't have time to plan anything carefully, but I don't want him to be able to talk to anyone else. There's one way to do it and with any luck kids will be blamed for it.

I hold my breath as I have to drive past the gypsy girl and her lover who are dawdling home from the dinner party. If they see me, I'll have to abort and do it another day, but I'm afraid I might not have another day.

Who knows what Sammy and Nancy are cooking up?

The village is empty when I get there. That's one good thing about the pub being closed; no-one is hanging about at this time of night. I park around the corner before walking to my destination.

My fingers are trembling as I light the fuse wire and push the fireworks through the letterbox. I dare not wait to hear them bang in case it wakes people up and they look outside to see what's going on.

I run back to my car and drive away towards Shrewsbury, knowing that hardly anyone will be coming from that direction. All I can do now is let the flames do their work . . .

* * *

Flames were reflected in all the windows when they reached the village centre. Several villagers had smelled the smoke and come out of their houses.

The lower floor of the pub was ablaze when Cara and Guy reached it.

'Mr Simpson,' Cara called on seeing him rushing out from his bungalow with a bucket of water. 'Have you seen Nancy?'

'No, Cara. There's no sign of her. The pub wasn't open again tonight. We hammered on the door and everything. I don't know what's up with the lass. I've called the fire brigade.'

'I've got the key,' said Cara, panic stricken. 'We should go in. She might be trapped.'

'I'll go, you stay here,' said Guy.

'I want to help.'

'Stay here and wait for the fire brigade,' he said, firmly. 'There's no point putting everyone in danger.'

'You might get hurt,' she protested.

'I'll be fine.' Guy pulled a big white handkerchief from his pocket and tied it around the lower half of his face.

Cara had an agonising wait as a few of the men went into the pub through the back door. Her mother had come up from their cottage, the news of the fire having travelled fast.

'Nancy might be in there Mum,' Cara said, her voice cracking. 'I don't understand. She's always so careful, making sure all the ashtrays are emptied, and the cigarette ends are put in water at the end of the night. She was always nagging me to remember to turn the stove off too. Oh, God, what if I left it on? What if it's my fault?'

Her guilt about leaving things in such a bad way with Nancy had got the better of her.

'I doubt it, sweetheart,' said Martha. 'You've had all your meals at home today, remember?'

'Yes.' Cara nodded. 'Oh, Mum, we hadn't made up properly.' She put her head on her mum's shoulder.

'Hush, now, she'll be fine, I'm sure.'

All around was confusion and chaos, as people tried to do their best to help. Some minutes later, there was a distant sound of a fire engine, which drew louder and closer. At the same time, Guy emerged from the pub, carrying someone wrapped in a blanket. The other men followed him, carrying a figure between them. It was a man, dressed in just his underpants and vest.

Guy put the person he carried on the floor, and knelt over them, giving mouth to mouth resuscitation. Cara moved nearer, and saw that it was Nancy. She was naked beneath the blanket.

The firemen started to douse the fire, while Guy worked frantically to bring Nancy back to life. An ambulance, an old Bedford left over from the war, came and two men jumped out. The local doctor had come from his house, and took over from Guy, trying to revive Nancy. His wife, who was a trained nurse, worked on the man, while everyone watched. It was as if the whole village was holding its breath.

Eventually they both looked up. The doctor spoke to those assembled.

'There's nothing more we can do. I'm sorry.'

Someone screamed, 'No! Nancy, no!'

Cara realised it was her. Loving arms surrounded her, before all went black.

* * *

'Do you want a cup of tea, love?' Martha sat on the edge of Cara's bed and took her hand. It was around two in the morning, and hardly anyone in Midchester seemed to have gone to sleep yet. Through the open curtains, Cara could see that there were lights on in nearly every house on the street.

After her initial shock she had become numb. She supposed it was a reaction to feeling too much pain over Nancy's loss.

'No thanks, Mum. I've had enough tea to sink a battleship.'

'Herbie has just come back. The firemen reckon someone threw a firework through the letterbox.'

'Who would do such a thing to

Nancy?' Cara asked.

'I don't know, sweetheart. But Herbie said that Mrs Abercrombie has identified the man with her as one of Nancy's boyfriends from a long time ago. He was always trouble that boy.' Unable to be unkind, Martha added, 'It wasn't his fault. His mum had a problem with drink, and he was neglected. I used to invite him here for meals sometimes, hoping our Freddie would make friends with him, but Sammy wasn't very bright, and you know our Freddie. He was really clever. He tried to be kind to Sammy, but they had nothing in common.'

'Sammy? Do you mean Sammy Granger?' With the shock of what had happened Cara had almost forgotten about the conversation at the dinner party.

'Yes, that's him.'

' Oh . . . ' Cara tried to get out of bed. 'I need to see Guy. I need to talk to him.'

'He's gone home to rest, and that's

what you should do.'

'But don't you see? There's a connection somewhere. At the dinner party, Mrs Abercrombie said she'd seen him the other day and Nancy met him. Then someone shoves a firework through the door of the pub. All that old, dry wood. They never stood a chance. Black must have guessed Sammy would go to stay with Nancy. That's what's been bothering her these last few days. Sammy came back to see her. I think I heard her talking to him this afternoon when I went for my clothes. I need to speak to Guy straight away.'

The words came out in a rush, as Cara jumped off the bed and started throwing some clothes on. She was breathless by the time she finished.

'Cara, love, it's past two in the morning. You can't go wandering up there alone this time of night.'

'I'll phone him then.'

'He'll be sleeping. He's had a busy night. Herbie said Guy did everything he could to save Nancy.'

'Yes, you're right. But Mum, what if Sammy knew something? Miss Watson said that she'd seen Sammy going up to Mr Black's house, but he acted as if he barely knew him.'

'Do you really think he might be Guy's brother-in-law?'

Cara had filled her mother in on their findings at the library when she had gone home to change before the dinner party.

'Guy doesn't recognise him, but he might be. He didn't look very happy when Reverend Cunningham offered to introduce Guy to his friend in intelligence. If she was hanged as a spy, then that might implicate Eric Black. If he's her husband, that is.'

'I don't know. He's been here a long time now.'

'Yes, over twenty years, but he didn't arrive here until after the war. He's not a villager.'

'Cara,' said Martha, reproachfully. 'I'm surprised at you, talking like that.

We're not from Midchester either. You should know better than to look down on people after the way we've been treated.'

'No Mum, I didn't mean it like that. What I mean is he wasn't born here, and has only been here since about nineteen-forty-four. We don't really know if anything he tells us about himself is true. He turns up and within a year he's running the newspaper and putting himself up as a councillor. Now he's our mayor, but we still don't know anything of his early life in Newcastle. And I overheard Miss Price saying that he's a possible parliamentary candidate in the next elections. He could end up as a Member of Parliament.'

'Being born in Newcastle doesn't make him a spy, Cara.'

'No, I know it doesn't, and there is the added problem that he claims to have been diabetic all his life. That could be a lie. But perhaps the German army didn't care about such things during the war as long as they had men fighting. Or maybe that's why he became a spy, because he wasn't able to fight. All we do know is that Greta came here for a reason, and it must have had something to do with her husband.'

* * *

The joint funerals took place several days later, on a dull, cold day in late October. Sammy had no living relative, and Nancy's only relation, Tom Yeardley was in America. He had been informed, but could not make the trip back in time. His daughter, Betty, had spoken to Cara on the telephone a couple of days before the funeral.

'He's devastated,' Betty said. 'He doesn't care about the pub, even though it's been in our family for years. He just can't imagine Midchester without Nancy. I've never known anything hit him this hard.'

'I'm having the same problem,' Cara had replied. 'I keep expecting to turn a corner and see her sauntering along the street in a mini skirt, with that fabulous red hair piled high on her head.' Every day since the fire began with the ache of remembering her best friend. 'Give Tom my love,' she said to Betty. 'I don't have to tell you to take care of him.'

'We're keeping a close eye on him, don't worry.'

Nearly everyone in the village turned out for the funerals, more for Nancy's sake than Sammy's. The pub had been the centre of the village. Most of the adults in Midchester had their first legal drink of alcohol in The Quiet Woman, either under Tom Yeardley's tenure or Nancy's. It was a special place to them, not just for the drink, but for the companionship they found there. Now it was gone, burnt to the ground. With it went a vivacious young woman who had listened to all their problems at some time or another.

'It's just too sad,' Mrs Simpson said at the graveside, adding, 'C'est la vie.' For once no-one rolled their eyes at her insistence on throwing French phrases into every sentence.

The police had put the fire down to a prank, blaming local teenagers. Neither Cara nor Guy believed that to be true, but — they realised they would have to be careful about slinging accusations. If there was a killer, it was better if they believed they had gotten away with it.

At the service, Reverend Cunningham talked about Nancy and her contribution to the village. He spoke of her vitality and good humour. He had less to say about Sammy Granger, because no-one knew what he had been doing since leaving the village. He did, however, touch upon Sammy's troubled younger life. When Cara saw Mrs Abercrombie nodding sadly, she guessed that the old headmistress had filled the vicar in on those details.

Cara looked across the grave and saw Eric Black, standing with Barbara Price. She felt an unaccountable burst of hatred for him, and had to remind herself that people were innocent until proven guilty. But since Guy told her on the way home from the dinner party that he believed Black to be a fake, she had started to notice it more. There was something too mannered in his performance. She noticed Barbara Price whispering in his ear, and for no good reason suspected that his lover was telling him how to look sad.

After the funerals the mourners went up to the village hall, where Cara and Meredith served tea and cakes. The atmosphere was understandably solemn as everyone sat around the tables, wondering who would be the first to speak.

'I could do with a drink,' said Len Simpson finally, looking down at his cup of tea. 'Any other funeral and we'd all go off to the Quiet Woman for a pint. Nancy'd cheer us all up.'

'That's not what you said when she first took over the pub,' his wife reminded him.

'Well, she had all that big hair and false eyelashes and those skirts that were more like belts,' Mr Simpson said. 'Besides, I always thought a pub needed a man at the helm. Not that I'm saying she did a bad job. She was a good lass.'

'She was that,' said Herbie Potter.

'The best,' said one of Mrs Simpson's friends.

Cara could not bear it any longer. She put her cup down with a clatter and ran outside, standing in the grounds of the village hall, wondering where to go next.

'You forgot your coat,' Guy said, putting it over her shoulders. He put his arms around her and instantly took away the chill she had been feeling.

'They used to criticise her all the time,' she said, jerking her head towards the village hall. 'Nothing she ever did was right. It was always This wouldn't have happened in Tom Yeardley's day', and 'When Tom Yeardley ran this pub'. Sometimes she'd cry about it at night, because she'd tried so hard to please them.' Cara rested her head against Guy's chest. 'She never cried for long though. She always bounced back and tried harder the next time.' She looked up at him. 'You didn't see her at her best, when she came home in a bad mood that time. She wasn't like that, not really.'

'I know,' Guy said softly. 'She had every right to be upset about me taking the pub over.'

'I think it's because you're a man, and she'd spent so long trying to bring them around to her way of doing things, then you turn up and in one night have them all eating out of your hand. You ought to have heard them when she put the jukebox in. They vowed never to use it and glared at anyone who tried. Then in one night they're all up and bopping away to the Rolling Stones.'

Guy hugged her closer. 'I'm sorry.'

'No, don't be. It's not your fault. You're you and I wouldn't want you any different.'

He smiled. 'Thank you. That's the nicest thing anyone has ever said to me.' He kissed her and it acted like a salve on the pain she felt, easing her tortured soul. She wished they were alone, so he could really bring her comfort. She wanted him desperately at that moment, wanted an end to the ache of loss.

There was a gentle cough behind them, and they looked around to see the Reverend standing nearby. 'Sorry,' he said, smiling kindly. 'I hate to disturb young lovers, but I need to speak to you, Guy. I've had word from my friend in intelligence and he said he's happy to talk to you. He's free on Saturday.'

'Thanks, Rev,' said Guy. He turned to Cara. 'Let's go down to London for the weekend. It'll do us good to get away from Midchester for a while.'

He was right. Midchester was too sad a place to be at that moment in time. The loss of Nancy and the pub hung like a thick, dark pall over everyone. Cara longed for spring when the sun would shine, and take away some of that darkness.

The Reverend gave Guy the details of his friend and where to find him in London. A few moments later, Meredith Cunningham joined them. 'I think we need to talk about the bonfire night celebrations,' she said.

'Do you think they should be cancelled?' asked Cara.

'Not completely, but perhaps we shouldn't have a bonfire. Not after what happened with the pub. I can't see anyone taking any pleasure in watching the flames. We could just have a few fireworks for the children, and a buffet in the village hall.'

'I agree,' said Cara.

'Shall we talk about it this weekend?' Meredith asked.

'Oh, I'm going to London with Guy this weekend, sorry.'

'That's fine,' said Meredith, looking at them both with the same shrewd eyes as her aunt. 'We'll talk about it when you get back. It won't need much alteration.'

People started leaving the chilly

village hall, wanting to get home. Actually they wanted to go to the pub, but that was impossible. Peg Bradbourne came out and joined them all.

'It's a sad business for Midchester,' she said. It was the first she had spoken all afternoon. Nancy's death seemed to have hit Peg harder than anyone, except for Cara. 'I've seen a lot in my time here. Midchester has had more than its fair share of murders, despite it only being a small place. But this . . . '

She shook her head, disbelievingly. 'Two people killed in the prime of their lives. It doesn't make sense. It's not teenagers or children either. The poor little beggars get blamed for everything around here. There's a wickedness in Midchester at the moment that goes beyond anything I've ever experienced. And yet, I can't say I haven't felt it before. I can never quite put my finger on it, but it's there, eating away at everyone.'

'You don't think it was an accident

either, do you, Peg?' asked Guy solemnly.

'No, Guy, I don't. Sammy ran away for some reason a long time ago, leaving the lass he loved behind. Because whatever else anyone might think of him, he loved Nancy. Then he comes back, and within days, he's dead, and so is she.'

She changed moods very quickly and said to Guy and Cara brightly, perhaps too brightly, 'Why don't you both come for tea tomorrow night?'

'We're off to London tomorrow,' Guy explained. 'We could come and see you when we get back.'

'Very well, but I want to know everything.'

Cara threw her arms around Peg, suddenly afraid it might be the last time she saw her. Losing Nancy had made her want to cling to all the other people she loved. 'Do be careful what you say to people about what you know, or what you think you know.'

'Oh, I haven't got to this age by being

careless, Cara. Don't you worry about me, my dear.'

Peg walked off down the path. At the gate leading to the village hall she stopped and looked at something on the ground, then picked it up and put it in her pocket.

At the same time, Eric Black, Barbara Price, Mrs Abercrombie and Miss Watson, along with several other villagers, stood watching Peg leave.

11

1966

I'd barely finished searching Anderson when I heard footsteps approaching. Damn it, why couldn't he have dropped dead further away from the houses? The path next to the village hall would have been ideal. I could have dragged him back there, but it meant moving out into the open. Even in the fog, I dared not risk it. I made a frantic grab for his notebook and bits of paper and moved as fast as I could.

I didn't realise it was her at first, I just knew that someone was coming and that I had to get off the street. I managed to duck down one of the alleys and hide. It was even darker there, so I was well hidden.

When she was close enough to see through the fog, I had to fight the compulsion to laugh. There was a sort of synchronicity to her being there. Is the gypsy girl going to haunt me forever? Or worse still, is she to be my downfall?

She's not a grubby little child anymore. She's a beautiful young woman, and like many others around here, I'm attracted to her. But that doesn't mean I didn't fear her and what she can do to me. I'm being ridiculous. There was no way she could connect Anderson with what happened before. She doesn't even know him.

Then the Sullivan man joined her. I was too far away to make out what they were saying to each other.

When people came out of the back of the houses, I had to keep my head down as I walked past, hoping and praying they wouldn't recognise me.

By the time I was able to walk around to the far end of the village and seem as if I'm just arriving with all the other onlookers, the police and ambulance were there and everyone else had gone up to the village hall.

I managed to keep out of sight, until I could hang around the village hall, waiting for someone to come out. She was there again, the little gypsy girl, and she seemed to think I was Sullivan. That was when I find out that he was searching Anderson's pockets.

Why would he do that? Unless he was the one who sent Anderson here . . .

Oxford Street was full of late night shoppers when Cara and Guy arrived in London on the Friday afternoon. They had booked into a hotel and then gone straight back out to take in the sights.

The Christmas lights were already up, giving everything a festive feel. Despite the sadness of the past week, Cara's spirits lifted. She had never been to London, so was taken by the glamour of it all. The change of scenery had done her good. They walked hand in hand to Soho, which was full of young men and women dressed in the type of fashions of which she could only dream. Though wearing a red sweater, with a black mini-skirt, knee-high boots and a sheepskin coat, she felt like a country mouse compared to them.

'You hold your own,' Guy said, as if reading her thoughts. 'Come on,' he said, 'I'll take you to the Marquee club. It's just around the corner.'

Cara had wanted to visit the Mary Quant shop, but hoped she could save that for another day. If she only went home with one Mary Quant mini-skirt, she would be very happy indeed.

'Do you know the Marquee club?' Guy asked.

'Of course I know of it. We do get music magazines in Midchester, you know. It's supposed to be the best club in London. All the best new bands play there. The Rolling Stones, The Who and loads more.'

He nodded. 'Yeah, that's what I'd heard. Let's hope there's a good group on tonight.'

The way the media spoke of the

Marquee club and the stars that frequented it, not just as performers but as punters, Cara had expected it to be very plush. Instead it was a jumble of plastic chairs, long tables and grubby looking booths. The carpet felt almost sticky underfoot as they walked across it. Cara did not like to think about what might have been spilled on it over the years. 'The village hall is better equipped than this,' she whispered to Guy as they waited to be served.

'Snob,' he teased. 'I show you the high-life and you're complaining about the décor. Mind you, in America places like this usually end each night with a police raid.'

'Really?' Cara half-hoped, half-dreaded that might be the case at the Marquee.

As it happened, hardly anyone sat on the chairs or at the table. Everyone stood shoulder to shoulder near to the front, nursing their drinks and waiting for the bands to play. Girls in mini-skirts and with no bra under their sheer blouses sidled up to young mods.

When the music started, Cara forgot all about the décor and just revelled in the music being played. Some of it was a little bit too psychedelic for her, but she loved the rhythm and blues bands. She had never seen a live group before, and had no idea just how exhilarating it could be. Forgetting all about Guy, she instinctively moved to the front and started dancing with all the other spectators.

When she finally remembered him, she turned around and saw him watching her with a smile on his face. 'What?' she mouthed at him.

'Nothing,' he mouthed back. He moved towards her and stood behind her with his arms around her waist. He whispered in her ear, 'You're only supposed to dance for me, remember?'

She turned to him and reached up, pressing her lips against his. The rest of the world drifted away. All she could think about was the taste and feel of him. 'Well, then we'd best go somewhere more private,' she suggested, lightly touching his mouth with hers.

It was cold outside, yet she hardly noticed, as they huddled close together on the way back to the hotel. The air was filled with anticipation. Cara's longing for him built up with each passing step.

They had booked two rooms, but as it turned out, she did not need hers. Guy unlocked the door to his and, taking her by the hand, beckoned her inside.

* * *

Hans? Guy Sullivan is Hans Mueller? He won't recognise me. Not after all these years. What if he does? He'll connect me to Greta. He'll realise she came looking for me, even if he does not suspect the reason.

Is it possible that after all this time my lies are unravelling? I've been careful. I've stayed in the background, guiding instead of leading. And now it's cost two more deaths. I don't care about that idiot Sammy, but I liked Nancy. She had colour whereas most of the villagers are grey. Sad that she became a casualty of war. Why couldn't the gypsy girl have been in the pub instead?

And then I saw that Peg Bradbourne had found something outside the village hall. I knew it came from Anderson's notebook. I recognised the size and shape of the paper. It must have fallen out and blown away when I searched him. Does it implicate me? Does it mention my name? None of the other notes did. He'd found out about Newcastle and Reginald Crumpler, but that doesn't matter so much.

If I have to abandon that sinking ship, I'll gladly do so. But I can't get away until I find out what else they know. There can be no danger of anyone coming looking for me.

I realised it was time to pay Peg Bradbourne a visit. She's stuck her nose into other people's business once too often.

I arrived at her house late at night, when the rest of the village are fast asleep. It's so easy to get into her little cottage. She doesn't even lock the back door at night, no-one around here does, not even during the war.

Where would she have put that paper? In her writing desk perhaps? That's the first place I look, but it's only full of letters to her sister, and old love letters from a beau who apparently died in the Great War. Then I check the waste paper bin. After all, she might not realise if there's anything significant on it.

I was just beginning to sort through the rubbish from the bin when she came through the sitting room door.

'Who's there?' she asked.

* * *

Cara woke up with a blissful smile on her face. She rolled over in bed and reached out for Guy, only to find an empty space. She heard the sound of the shower in the bathroom and mischievously thought about joining him when there was a knock at the hotel room door. She was not sure whether or not to answer, so she threw on some clothes and knocked on the bathroom door. After the night before, she realised she could have just walked in, but somehow the visitor at the door had made her feel shy about the whole situation.

'There's somebody at the door,' she said, knocking on the bathroom door.

'Can you get it?' he called back.

'Telegram for Mr Sullivan,' said the bellboy when Cara had answered. If he was shocked to find her there, good manners prevented him from showing it.

She found some change in her purse and gave it to him, wondering if she should give more, given the prestige of the hotel. He thanked her and left.

'You've got a telegram,' she called through the door. The shower stopped, and she heard movement, presumably as Guy dried himself.

'What does it say?'
'You want me to read it?'
'Yeah, why not?'
Cara opened the telegram. As she read the contents, her heart plummeted in her chest. She struggled to read it in calm tones. 'It says, Have come to Midchester. Stop. Need to see you urgently. Stop. All my love. Stop.'
The bathroom door flung open and Guy, wrapped in nothing but a bath towel, all but snatched the telegram from her. He read it as if he thought Cara might have left something out.
'We'll have to go back as soon as we've seen this Haxby man,' he said to Cara in business-like tones. 'You go and get ready, and I'll call and ask him to meet us earlier.'
'OK.' Cara did not know what else to say. It seemed that she was being dismissed. 'I'll get out of your way,' she added, through gritted teeth. She went to get the rest of her clothes. They seemed to be mocking her by the way they were strewn all over the floor. She

snatched them up, wanting this humiliating moment to be over.

As she left the room, she looked at him, willing him to say something to her to show he was still as interested in her as he had been when she was in his bed. He was too engrossed in reading the telegram to notice her.

The atmosphere as they walked through London to meet Richard Haxby was very different to the one of the night before. A few times Guy went to take Cara's hand but she pulled away. She had made a fool of herself over one man. She would not do it again over Guy Sullivan.

She had to accept things for what they were. It was nothing more than a one night stand, and while she did not like to think of herself as that type of girl, it was obviously all that Guy wanted. He probably saw her as a way of killing time until he was back with Selina Cartier or whoever it was who'd sent him the telegram. She had to behave as though it didn't matter.

So much for saying he was different to Tony Weston. Perhaps, in the end, all men were exactly the same.

Richard Haxby's office was in a discreet mansion near to the Houses of Parliament. Everything about the place said secret service. Guy made small talk as they waited, but Cara only answered him in monosyllables.

They were shown into Haxby's office, and Cara saw that everything about him said secret service too. He was a very handsome man, in his forties.

'It's good to meet you, Mr Sullivan. And you, Miss . . . ?'

'Baker. Cara Baker.' She stifled a nervous laugh when she realised she had just introduced herself in the same way as James Bond.

Richard Haxby grinned wryly. 'It's rather contagious, isn't it?' he quipped.

Cara thought that in different circumstances she could really fancy Richard Haxby. If she had not so stupidly gone and fallen in love with

Guy Sullivan. At that sudden realisation, she had to suppress a cry of agony. Luckily, neither Guy nor Haxby noticed.

'Haxby?' Guy raised an eyebrow. 'Any relation to James Haxby, the adventurer?'

'Yes, he's my father.'

'I've read about him,' said Cara. 'He and your mother have had some thrilling adventures.'

'And they haven't stopped, despite my best efforts to get them both to slow down,' said Haxby. 'Now, about the reason you came to see me.'

'I think Reverend Cunningham filled you in on all the details.'

'He did indeed.' Haxby turned to Cara as if an explanation were needed. 'Andrew and I were at university together, studying theology. I decided that being a vicar wasn't for me, so here I am. Though having met Andrew's wife, I'm kicking myself.'

'She is very lovely,' said Cara. 'She's a lovely person too.'

'Yes, I agree. Sorry,' he said to Guy.

'I looked into our files from that time, but any spies that were imprisoned or hanged at that time were named. There was no-one, even amongst those named, matching your sister's description. It's odd though.'

'What is?' asked Guy.

'There were rumours that someone was spying in that area. A man called Professor Solomon was arrested during the war, but very quickly cleared. It turned out that some local postman had a grudge against the American soldiers in the area. Oh, what was his name?' Haxby glanced through his notes.

'Herbie Potter,' Cara said, her voice barely above a whisper. 'He's my stepfather,' she told Haxby, ignoring Guy's shocked glance in her direction. 'His girlfriend ran off with an American airman and got pregnant. He knows what he did was silly.'

'People do strange things for love,' said Haxby kindly. 'I'm sorry if I've embarrassed you, Miss Baker.

'It's OK. So that was the only time you thought there was a spy in Midchester?'

'No, I was just getting to that. There have been rumours that someone was there, deeply undercover, but we've never found him. There were also a few dodgy five pound notes circulating for a while. We never tracked down the culprits, but we do know from experience that German spies often used forged currency. It was a way of hitting at morale, not to mention the economy.'

'What about Eric Black?' asked Guy. 'He's a fake if ever I saw one. I don't recognise him as my brother in law, but he could be. He's the right age.'

Haxby shook his head. 'We know all about Mr Black. We've had our eye on him for a while. He's a fake alright; claims to have come from Newcastle, where he was a big businessman. The bit about Newcastle is true but Eric Black began his working life as a housebreaker by the name of Reginald Crumpler. His trick was to break into houses during the blackout, when everyone else was safely inside their Anderson shelter. He did some time, and when he left prison he fell out of sight for a while. Our guess is that he hid some of his ill-gotten gains and used them to set up as a respectable businessman in Midchester. He thinks he's going to parliament, but I can assure you that's not going to happen. He'll be staying where he can't do any harm.'

'So if the hanged woman isn't my sister, what happened to her?' said Guy. It was a rhetorical question, but he sounded so unhappy that for a moment Cara forgot to be angry with him. She put her hand on his arm. He covered it with his.

'I did look into your brother-in-law's history,' said Haxby. 'His name was Frederick Schwartz, yes?'

'Yes, that's correct.'

'I'm sorry to say that he died during the Africa campaign. His name is listed amongst the dead, so it's very unlikely he got away from there and became a spy in Midchester.'

'Poor Brigitte,' said Guy. 'Whatever can I tell her? Her mother abandoned her, and never came home, and now we know her father is dead.'

'I'm sorry I couldn't give you better news,' said Haxby. 'But your sister was not a spy. I hope that gives you some comfort.'

'I'm not sure that it does, Mr Haxby. Because I still don't know what happened to her. I am very grateful to you for taking the time to look into this for me.'

'If you ever find out the truth, do let me know.'

'I will thank you.'

And with that, they were politely dismissed.

'I'm sorry,' said Cara, as they walked back to the hotel to collect their suitcases. 'I know you wanted definite news.'

'I will find out what happened to her, if it's the last thing I do,' said Guy, his lips set in a determined line. 'Come on, I have to get back to Midchester.'

Cara had almost forgotten that the sender of the telegram was waiting for him. They collected their things from the hotel, and made for the station. Guy barely spoke all the way home and Cara didn't feel like talking.

This was it. Soon the trip would be over, along with the brief moment of happiness she had enjoyed with Guy. She knew that she could never see him again, not even as an employee. It was too painful to be with him.

As soon as she reached Midchester, she would look for another job. She bit back the tears that threatened to fall. Not just for Guy, but for Nancy. She didn't know how much more heartache she could take.

They reached Midchester station in the early evening. It was already dark, and a mist had fallen over the town again. As they got down from the train, the light on the platform illuminated what could only be described as a vision. Cara recognised her immediately.

Selina Cartier stood on the platform, dressed in furs, with her platinum blonde hair shining under the lights. She was wearing far too much make up, especially around her eyes. Cara wondered what Guy could see in someone so overblown, but she supposed he was used to that, working with actresses.

'Guy,' Selina called, as they stepped down from the train. She ran to Guy and threw her arms around him. She spoke with a Southern Belle accent. 'Ah thought you'd never get here, and ah needed you!'

'It's alright, darling,' he said, holding Selina close and kissing her forehead. 'I'm back now and everything will be fine.'

They left the station together, leaving Cara standing alone with her bags. By some miracle her heart could survive a whole lot more breakage, which was a pity as she would have quite liked to die at that moment.

Somehow she managed to pick up her bags and put one foot in front of the other.

Martha Potter understood as soon as Cara got home.

'I heard Selina Cartier is here,' she said, as Cara threw her luggage down in the kitchen. 'That Enid woman told Mr Fletcher at the shop.'

She took Cara in her arms, instinctively knowing that she needed a hug.

'Oh, mum, I've been so stupid,' said Cara, bursting into tears. 'Again!'

'No,' said Martha, hugging her daughter tighter. 'He's the one who's been stupid.'

* * *

Martha did what she always did when Cara was in pain; sat her at the kitchen table, filled her up with tea, insisted she ate a plateful of egg and chips with a doorstep-sized chunk of bread and butter, then sat in silence until Cara was ready to talk.

Because her feelings for Guy were too raw, Cara pushed her plate away and told her mum about the meeting with Richard Haxby instead.

'So the mayor used to rob houses?' was all Martha could say. 'Fancy that. I always knew there was something about that man. Then again, he's done well for himself since, I'll give him that much.'

'But it's all based on lies, mum. He preaches to us all about crime prevention, and yet we've been in more danger of him breaking into our houses.'

'Oh!' Martha exclaimed, throwing her hands up in the air. 'That reminds me. Poor old Peg got broken into last night.'

'Oh God, is she alright? Did she get hurt?'

'She's fine. She disturbed whoever it was, and they ran away. She's staying at the vicarage for now. Reverend Cunningham wouldn't hear of her staying home alone. She said she wanted to see you.'

'Maybe I'll walk up there. She said she wanted to see us . . . but I suppose Guy has other concerns now.'

'It's getting a bit late, sweetheart. Go tomorrow when you've had time to rest.'

'Perhaps you're right,' Cara conceded reluctantly.

'I'm always right. I'm your mother.'

'You're the best. You always forgive people, Mum.'

'I forgive you because you have such a hard time forgiving yourself, Cara. You're young. You're allowed to make mistakes.'

'I can't help thinking that if I hadn't packed my job in with Nancy, I'd have been there with her and she might have lived.'

Martha's eyes brimmed with unshed tears. 'Yet I've been thanking God every day that you weren't at the pub that night. You might not have lived, and I can't even bear to think of that. I think Nancy had a reason to tell you it was time you moved on. She was keeping you safe from whatever trouble Sammy was in, I'm sure of it.'

'I wish she'd kept herself safe.'

'Ah, but as you know, my darling, when it comes to men, women are seldom sensible.'

'Gee, thanks, Mum. I feel so much better now.' Despite that, Cara managed to laugh.

'That's better. In a few weeks' time, Guy Sullivan will be long gone and you'll forget about him.'

Cara was not so sure about that. She was just about to go up to bed when the telephone rang.

'Hi, Cara, it's Guy. Look, I'm so sorry for wandering off and leaving you at the station. I should have seen you home safely.'

'Don't worry about it. I didn't have far to walk.'

'Even so, I'm sorry, Cara. Things are a bit hectic up here, but that's no excuse for my bad manners.'

Cara did not know what to say to that. That last thing she wanted to think about was Guy having hectic reunion sex with Selina Cartier.

'Are you still there?' he asked.

'Yes, I'm still here. Like I said, don't worry. You obviously had more important things to deal with.'

'You're important to me too, Cara. I do worry about you.'

'Well don't. I'm a big girl and I can take care of myself.'

'Can I see you tomorrow? I want to talk to you.'

'Erm, no, sorry. I have to go and see Peg.'

'I'll come with you. She said she wanted to see us both.'

'No, that's not a good idea. I think she has her own concerns at the moment. Her house was broken into last night.'

'Is she OK?'

'Mum says she is. I'll know more tomorrow.'

'Well, keep me posted, will you? She's a nice old lady.'

'Yeah, of course. Goodnight.'

She put the phone down then went to bed and had disturbing dreams about Guy passionately kissing Selina Cartier. Then the scene shifted to the village hall and Peg picking up slips of paper before someone came up behind her and hit her on the head.

12

I should have killed the old woman when I had the chance. She was there, in front of me. I don't know what stopped me. It certainly wasn't affection for her. Maybe it was self-preservation.

As far as I know, what happened to Sam and Nancy might be put down to a schoolboy prank. But if I hit Peg Bradbourne over the head with a hammer during a break in, someone might start questioning why there were so many murders in Midchester in such a short space of time. Soon those questions will come to my door and I may have to account for myself.

I had to run before she saw me clearly, without knowing what was on that slip of paper. There's nothing else for it. I have to get away from Midchester. But how? I dare not get in touch with my old contacts in Germany. Besides, they're all a bunch of turncoats. How quickly they capitulated when Berlin fell, covering their tracks and pretending they had no choice. And after all the things I've sacrificed for the Fatherland . . . Greta . . . oh darling, foolish Greta. I should make a new start, somewhere else, where no-one knows me. I've done it before, I can do it again.

* * *

On Sunday morning, Cara received a phone call from Peg, asking her to visit and suggesting she should go up to the vicarage while the vicar and Meredith were at the church.

'We can have a nice quiet chat,' Peg said when Cara arrived at around ten-thirty.

Peg fussed around in the vicarage kitchen, making tea and putting chocolate digestives onto a plate.

'Are you all right, Peg?' asked Cara.

'Mum said you disturbed the burglar, but she didn't mention if you were hurt.'

'Oh I'm fine, my dear. You look a little pale.'

'I'm just tired from travelling,' said Cara. She held out her hands for the tea tray.

'Thank you, Cara. Take it into the sitting room. We won't be disturbed there.'

When they were seated, Peg insisted Cara tell her everything about what they had learned from Richard Haxby. Cara could manage that, but she avoided Peg's more searching questions about herself and Guy.

'So the Mayor was a burglar, eh? We always knew there was something, but couldn't quite work out what.'

'Why did everyone vote for him in the local elections, Peg?'

'I don't know . . . It's a strange thing. When I think back to his speeches, they always sounded so rousing. But since I've had more time to think about them, I realise he actually said very little at all. Like Hitler.'

'I don't think he's Hitler, Peg. He isn't even the German spy they think has been hanging around here for a while.'

'Yes, I wonder who that could be. Most of the men around here were born here, apart from Eric Black. And my nephew-in-law, Andrew Cunningham.'

'I don't think the vicar is a spy, do you?'

'He has those Aryan good looks that Germans go so wild about, but no, I think Andrew is definitely one of us.'

'What about Mr Simpson?' Cara ventured.

'Len! No, he hasn't got the brains to be a spy. Not that he isn't a good, hard-working man.'

'Herbie?' Cara suggested quietly.

'No, dear girl. Herbie isn't all that bright either.'

'Oh, but he is, Peg. Mum says he has hidden depths.'

'Somehow I don't think she's talking about his intellect.'

'Peg!' Cara could not help laughing. 'I know what Herbie did during the war was silly, but he's not a bad man either.'

'No, he isn't. And he did a good thing, taking on your mother and five children.'

'I wish I'd appreciated him more at the time. I think I've probably been really ungrateful to him. I ran rings around him when I was a teenager.'

'Then he was a real father to you,' said Peg, with a smile.

'Nancy knew something, I'm sure of it. The afternoon before she died she told me that there might be things about Guy's sister that even he didn't know about. I took it to mean that Greta was a spy, but now I wonder if she meant something else entirely. If only we knew why Sammy ran away.'

'Oh, but we do, dear,' said Peg, taking a sip of her tea.

'Do we?'

'Well, we do now. Mr Fletcher told

me about it the other day. One day, back in nineteen-forty-six, Sammy went into his shop to buy cigarettes. After he'd paid for them and gone away, Mr Fletcher found out the five pound note was forged. He called in the police and everything. It wasn't the first time it had happened you see. I think Sammy must have realised he was in trouble, and then run away.'

'Mr Haxby said something about forged notes, Peg. He said there had been a few, but they didn't track down the culprit. He thinks the Germans did it to undermine the economy and hit at morale. We need to find out where Sammy got that note.'

'Yes, that would help, but I can't imagine who would know.'

'What about one of his friends from that time? He might have said something to them about it.'

'Let me see? Who was he running around with then? There was your brother, Freddie, of course.'

'Yes, but mum said they never really

hit it off. I don't think Freddie would know. I could ask him, I suppose.'

'Freddie might have told your mother, Cara?'

'No, not if Sammy asked him not to. Freddie can be really secretive about things.'

'Yes, so I've heard,' said Peg, wryly. 'Does he still share a flat with Ralph?'

'Yes, he does,' Cara said with mock sternness. 'Yes, maybe I'll give him a ring. I suppose I should be getting back. Oh, Peg, I forgot. When we were coming away from the village hall the other day I saw you pick something up from the ground.'

'I wondered when you were going to ask me about that,' said Peg, with a secretive smile.

'Why? Is it important?'

'I don't know, but I noticed everyone looking. It was just a scrap of paper with one question written on it.'

'What question?'

'It said 'Who is Lotte?''

'Lotte? Guy mentioned his sister

having several friends called Lotte. I suppose Mr Anderson heard the name and didn't know the connection with Greta Mueller.'

'Or,' said Peg, sipping her tea with a benign expression, 'he might have been wondering who in Midchester was Lotte.'

Cara's eyes widened in surprise. 'You think one of the Lottes is here? I suppose that would explain why Greta ended up here. I ought to go and see Guy and tell him.'

'You said that very reluctantly, Cara. I thought you and Guy were getting close.'

'Selina Cartier was waiting for him at the station last night,' said Cara, miserably.

'So I heard,' said Peg.

'How can you have heard that, Peg? It was late yesterday evening and hardly anyone else was there.'

'There's always someone about in Midchester,' said Peg. 'Meredith's cleaning lady was collecting her son from the station. He's in the army, you know. Anyway, she told me when she arrived this morning. She says Miss Cartier is very beautiful, but wears far too much make up.'

'She shovels it on with a trowel, I think. Oh no, I shouldn't be bitchy,' said Cara. 'She is very beautiful.'

'In my day there was only one reason a woman wore that much make up.'

'Because she was a prostitute?' said Cara, unable to resist another catty remark at Selina Cartier's expense.

Peg laughed, but there was sadness in her eyes. 'No, dear, because she was hiding something far worse. A black eye or a bruised nose.'

'Oh, you mean her husband hits her?' Shame-faced, Cara looked down at her tea. 'Now I feel rotten. I suppose that's why she turns to Guy. But why doesn't she just leave her husband?'

'It's very difficult to switch off your love for someone, even if they are cruel to you.'

'You sound as if you speak from

experience, yet you've never married, have you?'

'No, but it doesn't mean I haven't experienced falling in love with the wrong man.'

'I seem to make a habit of that,' said Cara. 'Though no-one has ever hit me, so I suppose I should be grateful for that.'

'There are other ways a man can wound a woman. He doesn't need to use his fists.'

'I know,' Cara said, remembering how she felt when Guy ushered her out of the hotel room. She found herself telling Peg all about it.

'I used to tell Nancy all this type of thing,' she explained. She remembered late nights when she sat on the edge of Nancy's bed, sharing all her secrets, and it grieved her to think she would never be able to do that again. 'But I couldn't tell mum because I was afraid she would be disappointed in me. And now I suppose you think I'm cheap and awful.'

'I think no such thing,' said Peg. 'Shame on Guy for making you feel that way. If he cheapened what should have been a special night that was his problem, Cara, not yours. I also know Martha well enough to know she would never be disappointed in you. She has a very forgiving soul, has Martha.'

'Yes, I know. I was only saying the other day that I wish I was more like her. Though I don't think I can ever forgive Guy for yesterday morning.'

'Oh, you might, if he turns up and says all the right things,' said Peg, with that familiar twinkle in her eye.

Cara shook her head vehemently. 'No. I'm off men for good.' She was a bit disconcerted when Peg burst out laughing.

'Anyway,' said Peg, when she was more composed. 'I suppose I had better give you this to take to Guy.' She slipped her hand into her cardigan pocket and pulled out the piece of paper. 'He should know about it, even if you are angry with him.'

'Yes, I know. With any luck he'll soon find out what happened to Greta then he'll go back off to Hollywood or Australia and I'll never have to see him again.'

'The day you can say that and look happy about it is the day I know you're really over him.'

'I'm a hopeless case, aren't I?' Cara said, smiling sadly.

'Oh no, Cara.' Peg shook her head solemnly. 'I've always had very high hopes for you, my dear.'

Cara left Peg at the vicarage and went home to place a call to her brother, Freddie. Ralph answered and said that Freddie was out, but that he would ask him about Sammy Granger as soon as he got home.

She decided to walk up to the Grange. She would have to face Guy sometime and it was better to get things over with. She also resolved to show him that she did not care about Selina Cartier. She would be composed and friendly, and then he would not have the satisfaction of having hurt her.

Her resolve trembled slightly when she knocked on the door of the Grange and Selina Cartier appeared. She had been expecting Enid to answer.

'Cara?' she said with a smile.

'That's right,' she replied, formally. 'I wondered if I could see Mr Sullivan, please. I have some information to share with him about his sister.'

'I'm so glad to meet you properly.'

Cara looked at Selina and frowned. The southern belle accent had gone to be replaced by a faint Australian twang. The make-up and coiffured wig had also gone. In their place was a fresh faced young woman, with pretty blue eyes and natural blonde hair, who was only a few couple of years older than Cara. There was also the hint of a bruise around her eye, which brought to mind what Peg had said.

'Come on in, Cara. Guy is just getting dressed, but I wanted to have a chat with you anyway.'

Oh dear, thought Cara, following

Selina to the drawing room. *Is this the bit where you tell me to lay off your boyfriend?*

'Please sit down. Can I get you anything? Tea? Coffee?' Selina was wringing her hands and looked even more nervous than Cara felt. She sat down on the sofa and curled up. Cara took one of the chairs.

'No, thank you. What did you want to talk to me about? If it's about me and Guy . . . '

'Oh, look, I'm so sorry, Cara. It was really selfish of me to turn up and drag him away like that. We left you all on your own. I can't begin to imagine how you felt.'

'Well, I'm sure that as you haven't seen each other for a long time . . . ' said Cara, completely flummoxed by the way the conversation was going. Selina seemed so humble and, well, nice. Cara hardly knew what to make of it. Maybe Guy had lied to Selina too.

'Actually, I saw Uncle Hans just before he left for Midchester, but I had problems and needed a friend. He's my best friend. He's the only one who really looks out for me.'

'Uncle Hans? Sorry, but who are you? I thought you were Selina Cartier.'

'That's who the world thinks I am but actually I'm Brigitte. Brigitte Schwartz.'

13

'You're Greta's daughter?' Cara could hardly believe it. Guy had mentioned searching for Brigitte, and saving her from an abusive marriage, but never once had she associated his niece's story with that of Selina Cartier.

'That's right,' said Brigitte. 'Uncle Hans — I'll have to remember that you know him as Guy — has been trying to find her for me. I just want to know what happened.'

Brigitte's pretty eyes filled up with tears. 'I know she wouldn't have abandoned me, but it's the not knowing what happened that's worse. You know?'

'Yes, of course, I'm so sorry, Brigitte. But I don't understand. There were stories in the paper about you and Guy.'

'Oh, I know. It's so embarrassing.

We're going to put that right, just as soon as I find out what happened to Mama. It's a long story. Do you mind if I tell it to you?'

'No, not at all. In fact I'd be grateful if you did because I'm completely confused at the moment.'

'I ran away from home and got married at the age of fifteen. My first husband was an American so we lied about my age and hopped on a ship to America. When we got there, I found out that the big businessman I had married actually lived in a two room shack in Los Angeles with his parents and three brothers.

'I tried, I really did, but he drank and he was unkind to me. I walked out, got divorced and a friend helped me to get a bit part in a film. It turned out I was quite good at it, and the next thing I know, I'm famous. That's when I became Selina Cartier. I reinvented myself as a southern belle from some faded gentry.

'Uncle Hans — Guy — found me

about eight years ago, and not a moment too soon. I'd married a film producer by then. He was good to me at first, but then when his films started failing he took it out on me. He was a real psychopath, so Guy got me away from him. Unfortunately, there was a reporter watching my house and we were seen leaving together. The next thing we know, they're saying that we've eloped.'

'Why not just say you were his niece?'

'We'd both come up with different back stories, you see. I was the southern belle and Guy was the lanky Australian outback man who'd worked his way across America. We'd have had to admit we were both German and that's not a good idea. Especially not with McCarthy breathing down everyone's necks at the end of the fifties, looking for communists. You know what a witch hunt that was.'

Cara nodded. She had been quite young at the time, but she had read about it.

'Communists, Nazis,' Brigitte continued. 'They're all the same to Americans, especially now that our part of Berlin is behind the Iron Curtain. So anyway, that's how it all came about. I'm so sorry if I let you get a different impression last night. I really wasn't thinking.'

'And you've been hurt again,' Cara said gently looking pointedly at Brigette's eye. It was a statement, not a question.

Brigitte nodded. 'Oh, I certainly know how to pick them,' she sighed. 'They always seem so nice to begin with but then . . . I'm off men for good.'

Cara laughed but there was a bitter taste to it. 'I was just saying the same to a friend.'

'Really?' said Brigitte, frowning. 'But Guy . . . Oh, well, perhaps I should let him talk to you about that.'

As if on cue, the door to the drawing room opened.

'Cara, there you are,' Guy said. He smiled, looking genuinely pleased to see her. 'I've just been in the study, ringing your house and talking to your mum.

Did you see Peg?'

Oh, she thought, *that's why he's pleased to see me*. She still felt the pain of his abrupt behaviour of the previous morning. That Selina turned out to be his niece, Brigitte, did not really alter what happened. He'd still made her feel cheap and nasty.

'Yes, I did. She found what seems to be a bit of Anderson's notebook.' Cara handed him the sheet of paper.

Guy read it out. 'Who is Lotte?'

'You said there were several Lottes,' said Cara. 'Could it be one of her friends?'

'No, Uncle Hans,' said Brigitte, chipping in. 'There was only one Lotte.'

'How on Earth do you know, sweetheart?' asked Guy. 'You weren't even born then.'

'Mama used to talk about her all the time. She was Mama's most special friend.'

'What?' Guy's face went pale. 'When did Greta say that?'

'Oh loads of times. She said I'd meet

her one day and she'd be my special friend too.'

Guy sat down on the sofa quickly, as though he had been punched in the gut. 'I'm sure you're wrong. There was more than one Lotte.'

'Mama said that Lotte used to like dressing up and fooling people. It's funny, but Mama reckoned that Lotte could never fool you, no matter how much she changed her look. Maybe that's why you thought there was more than one.'

'Yes, maybe,' said Guy distantly. He turned to Cara. 'Is it possible we've been looking at this all the wrong way, Cara?'

'I'm not sure what you mean,' said Cara — but it was beginning to dawn on her.

'I mean if Lotte was Greta's *special* friend, maybe she's the reason that Greta came to Midchester.'

'Peg said that the question could mean which one of the villagers was Lotte.' Cara paused, not sure how to proceed. The conversation had become very awkward. 'Before she died, Nancy said there may be things about your sister that you didn't know. I'm sorry, Guy, but I didn't say anything because I didn't want to upset you. Anyway, I just thought Nancy meant Greta was a spy and that somehow Sammy had found out.'

'Hang on a minute,' said Brigitte. 'Are you both thinking that Mama and Lotte were close? Like lovers?'

'Yes,' said Guy. 'In fact, it all makes more sense now. It was a surprise to the family that Greta married at all. She'd shown no interest in men. Then she met your father and we all supposed it was just that she'd met the right bloke at last. Maybe that wasn't it at all. I'm sorry, Brigitte, I know this must be upsetting for you.' He reached over and squeezed her hand.

'No more upsetting than thinking she might have died because of it,' said Brigitte. She rubbed her swollen eye as if it had suddenly started hurting again. 'In which case there's nothing wrong with Mama's feelings — only the person she shared them with.'

'I'd best go,' said Cara, feeling she was intruding. 'I'll leave you both to talk things over. Guy there was something else. Remember Richard Haxby saying that there were forged notes circulating in Midchester?'

'Yes?'

'Sammy had one of them. I'm going to call my brother, Freddie, later in case Sammy said anything to him about it. But it does suggest that Sammy knew who the spy was. Anyway, I'd better be going.'

'I'll walk you to the door,' said Guy.

'It's OK, I'll see myself out.'

Guy ignored her and insisted on seeing her to the door. Cara saw Brigitte smile encouragement at him as they left the room.

'Cara,' said Guy, when they were alone in the hallway. 'I am sorry about last night, truly.'

'Yes, you already said,' she replied in cool tones.

'So why are you still angry with me? If it's about Brigitte, I think she's explained everything to you.'

'You could have told me yourself.'

'Yes, I know. I was waiting for the right time, that's all.'

'The right time was before you ushered me out of your room like I was some cheap trollop.'

'Cara, I didn't mean to treat you like that.'

'Well, it's the way you made me feel,' she said. 'If all you were interested in was a one night stand, that's fine. I don't expect hearts and flowers. But to treat me like something you throw out with the rubbish . . . '

'Is that all it was for you? A one-night stand?'

'I . . . well, yes . . . I suppose so. I don't know what it was. I thought it was special.'

'Of course it was special.' He reached over and moved a stray strand of hair from her face. 'I had a really good time.'

'Well that's me,' said Cara bitterly. 'A regular good time girl.' With that she yanked open the door and took off down the path.

Well that was mature, she thought to herself.

But barely a moment later, Guy caught her by the arm.

'Have you any idea what I've been going through these past few weeks?' he said, his face a mask of fury. 'My sister might have been murdered and my niece keeps getting involved with men who abuse her. Then I get a telegram from her when I'm miles away and can't do anything to comfort her. But of course none of that is important as long as I make Miss Cara Baker feel good! Just because some idiot a few years ago treated you like a slut doesn't mean every man is the same if he's not telling you how wonderful you are every second of the day!'

Cara wanted to die of shame. He was right. Of course, he was right. She had been selfish in forgetting the real reason Guy was in Britain. Added to which he must have been worried sick when he got Brigitte's telegram. But none of that excused what he had just said to her.

'I'm very sorry,' she said, choking back tears. 'I do realise things have been bad for you, but I've also lost someone in the past couple of weeks. My best friend died, possibly because she or Sammy knew something about your sister.'

'Oh Cara . . . '

'No, it doesn't matter. I'm not saying it's your fault it happened. It just did.' She sniffed loudly. 'You know, I did feel good about myself when I was with you. You helped me to forget what had happened to Nancy for a little while, and I'm grateful for that. I just didn't realise I would be dismissed so abruptly. But as you say, you have other concerns, so please don't let me keep you from them any longer.'

'Cara . . . ' Guy ran his fingers

through his hair in frustration. 'I'm sorry.'

'Don't bother to apologise, Guy. Because as cheap as Tony made me feel, he never hurt me the way you just did.'

She dashed away before he could stop her again and ran down the driveway, refusing to look back. Peg had been right. A man did not have to hit you to wound you beyond repair.

* * *

Cara didn't want to go home crying yet again. It would only worry her mum, so she wandered around the outskirts of the village until she felt calmer.

She had always known that it would not last with Guy. Even without someone like Selina Cartier in the picture, Cara knew that she was nothing like the sort of women he normally associated with. She fooled herself into believing that she could be sophisticated, like the fashionable girls in London, who moved happily from one relationship to another.

A few weeks earlier she would have insisted that she was a very modern young woman. Now she realised that she was old-fashioned at heart. No matter how much she had tried to pretend she could have a casual affair with Guy, deep down her heart had always been involved.

It seemed to her that having sex so casually must eventually chip away at one's soul. At least that was how she felt. She didn't know if she would give up men. Hearing Brigitte say it had brought home how ridiculous she had sounded when she said the same to Peg at the vicarage. But she made a vow to be more careful in future. She would not rush into a relationship again.

Her impetuous streak always seemed to get her into trouble. First with walking out of the pub in a huff just before Nancy died, and then with losing her temper with Guy. So much for being cool, calm and collected. She'd behaved no better than a stroppy ten-year-old and both times it had cost her dearly.

Perhaps it was time to leave Midchester. Being in London had shown her a completely different world; one where she could start behaving as an adult. In London she would not have to worry about the nosey neighbours watching her and commenting on her every move. They still saw her as the grubby little gypsy girl. The biggest problem was that a lot of the time, that's how she saw herself. There was no escape from it in Midchester. But in London no-one would know or care where she came from.

With her mind made up and her tears dried, she made her way back to the centre of the village.

'Cara!' Brigitte was standing near to Mr Fletcher's sweet shop. 'I've been looking all over for you.'

'I've been for a walk,' she said, crossing the road to Brigitte. 'Is anything wrong?'

'No, I just wanted to chat to you

again, without Guy around. He's been in a foul mood since you went off earlier. He's such a baby sometimes,' said Brigitte.

She put her arm in Cara's and they walked along the street together. It was as if they had been friends forever, which Cara found a bit strange. But she liked Brigitte, so she didn't mind too much. 'He's like all men,' Brigitte continued. 'They never can say the right thing, and then they sulk because they think we've misunderstood them.'

'I don't think I misunderstood him,' said Cara sadly.

'He's been under a lot of pressure,' said Brigitte. 'That's partly my fault because of how I messed up my life. He's been looking after me and Grandma for so many years and he had to grow up long before he should have, what with Mama gone and Grandpa dead.'

'I know,' said Cara. 'Well, I don't know, but I can imagine.' She felt worse than ever. Brigitte clearly adored Guy.

'So does that mean you'll forgive him?'

'Oh, I don't know about that, Brigitte. Anyway, I don't know what you think, but your uncle and I just had some fun together, that's all. It was nothing more than that.'

'I see.' Brigitte nodded sagely. 'That must be why he has a face like thunder and when I saw you walking down the road, you looked like someone kicked your puppy.'

Cara could not help laughing at that. 'I know what you're trying to do, Brigitte. But please don't. This is between me and Guy. I don't think anything you say or do is going to make any difference.'

'You don't know how determined I can be.'

'I think I do. You ran away to America when you were fifteen. That shows determination. I wish I had the courage to do the same. I was just thinking about moving to London. It's time I got out of Midchester.'

'Why? It's a nice little village. Everyone has been really kind to me. Even Uncle's Hans's assistant, Enid and she's usually so disapproving.'

'You're Selina Cartier, movie star. Of course, they're nice to you. Sorry, that wasn't fair. You're a sweetheart in your own right too. Why don't you come to my house and meet my mum? I'm sure she'd love to see you. If you haven't got anything better to do.'

'I'd love to meet your mum. Guy says she's great, and that your house is just like grandma's. I really miss her.

'When was the last time you saw her?'

'A couple of months. She lives outside of Hollywood, and I'm always working. That's a lame excuse I know. I really ought to see her more, but I think it upsets her.'

'Why?'

'Because I look so much like my mother. At least when I'm not all made up as Selina.'

'Oh.'

They had reached Cara's garden gate, when Martha came out of the house.

'Mum, this is . . . ' Cara paused, not knowing how to introduce her companion.

'Brigitte Schwartz,' said Brigitte. 'Guy's niece.'

'Oh, you dear girl,' said Martha, opening the garden gate and practically sweeping Brigitte into her arms. 'What a dreadful time you must have had. Let me put the kettle on. Are you hungry? I can do some egg and chips if you want.'

'I haven't had egg and chips for absolutely ages,' said Brigitte. 'I'd love some!'

As Brigitte spoke, Cara heard a loud metallic crash.

She turned and saw a car had crashed into a tree just outside the house. A bloodied figure got out and headed for her in a blaze of fury. All she could do was stand and gape as big hands surrounded her throat.

14

I couldn't stop thinking about the gypsy girl. She's haunted my steps throughout this. First as a child and now as an adult.

She knows about me, I'm sure of it. She's been talking to Peg Bradbourne and Guy Sullivan about me. If anyone proves to be my undoing, it will be her. I've always known that.

I saw how pensive she looked at the dinner party. She must have felt my hatred burning into her soul. All the times I've had to smile and encourage her in her writing endeavours. She was nothing but a dirty little gypsy, and no amount of education is going to change that.

With my hatred of the girl growing stronger by the minute, I decided to go down to the village and drive past her house. It might help me to decide how I was going to deal with her. Because there was no way I would leave Midchester while that girl was still breathing.

I was driving past when I saw her in the garden.

Greta!

I lost control of the car and it crashed into a tree, but I barely felt the pain as my head hit the steering wheel.

She'd come back to me. Greta was here, looking as beautiful as ever. She had forgiven me. We can be together.

Even as I got out of the car, the gypsy girl's witch of a mother was holding Greta by the arm and taking her away from me.

Damn them!

I will kill that gypsy girl if it's the last thing I do.

* * *

A couple of hours later, Cara sat in the chair, nursing her sore throat. Barbara Price had been dragged from her, but not before doing some serious damage to her wind-pipe. The police had come and taken Price away for questioning.

Martha Potter's sitting room was crowded with visitors. Guy and Brigitte were there, along with Peg Bradbourne. Richard Haxby had come up from London by helicopter. Even Eric Black was visiting and Martha and Herbie were on hand to give everyone tea and biscuits.

'I had no idea,' Black was saying. 'I swear to it.'

Somehow Cara believed him.

'She was very clever,' said Richard Haxby. 'Her name was Lotte Schmidt. She used to be an actress in Germany.'

'That will explain all the disguises,' said Guy. 'And why I thought there was more than one Lotte.'

'Yes, that's quite right,' said Haxby. 'She was an expert at creating different looks. From what we've been able to piece together since all this came to light, she moved to Britain in nineteen-thirty-nine, just before war broke out.

Her grandmother was British so she could speak English without an accent. She was able to settle in Midchester, working for the land army.'

'That's what she was doing when I first met her,' said Black. 'When I told her about my political ambitions, she attached herself to me. Not that I minded. She was a very attractive woman.' He paused. 'I loved her. Foolish, I know, but there you go and I wouldn't be where I am today without her.'

'Hmm,' said Haxby. 'We'll discuss that later, Mr Crumpler.'

Black turned ashen. 'So you know all about that then? Look, I just wanted to make a clean start that's all. And I thought Barbara could help me. True she had some strange ideas, but I always ignored them, because when it came to rallying the people, she knew what she was talking about.'

Richard Haxby shrugged and continued with his story.

'She was never quite the spy she

thought she was. She passed on some secrets about the air base but as we didn't run sorties from there, it wasn't much help. She circulated some dodgy notes, but it didn't do much to affect the economy. My guess is that she was left here to rot. Her fanaticism was too much even for the Nazi party, which is saying something. We gather there was a history of mental illness in the family. That and having to hide her true sexuality . . . well it all went to creating the woman we know as Barbara Price and the woman Greta Mueller knew as Lotte Schmidt. I'm sorry if this is distressing for you, Miss Mueller.'

Cara noticed that Richard Haxby was very taken with Brigitte.

'I'm just glad I know the truth at last,' said Brigitte. 'Do you know what happened to my mother?'

'Not yet. We're still questioning Miss Price, but as soon as we find out, I will let you know.'

'Can I talk to her?' Brigitte asked. 'With me looking so much like Mama, I might be able to persuade her to tell me.'

'It could be very distressing for you.'

'More distressing than thinking my mother abandoned me twenty years ago?'

'Point taken, Miss Mueller. I'll see what I can do.'

'Will you come too, Cara?' Brigitte asked.

Guy looked a little bit put out and Cara whispered, unable to speak properly, 'Perhaps you should take your uncle. After all, he has a right to know too.'

'I meant for you to come with both of us,' said Brigitte. 'I wouldn't leave Uncle Hans out.'

'I think Cara should be resting,' said Guy. 'And Barbara has already attacked her once. We don't know if she'll do it again.'

Taking it as a sign that he didn't want her there, Cara nodded. 'Yes, I think that's for the best. Besides,' she added, struggling to speak, 'it might prevent her from speaking if I'm there. Perhaps you can come and tell me about it afterwards, Brigitte.'

'We both will,' said Guy, frowning. 'That is if we're both welcome.' He emphasised the 'both'.

'Of course,' said Cara. She took a sip of tea, as much to soothe her throat as to hide the sob that lingered there. This was not about her now. It was about Guy and Brigitte finding out the truth about Greta. 'I'd like to know what happened to your sister, if you don't mind telling me.'

'Come and see her tomorrow,' said Martha. 'I'm not going to allow her to speak for the rest of the day. If I had my way she would be in hospital.'

'Yes, you're quite right,' said Guy. 'Perhaps we could drop you off there on the way, Cara. You should get that throat checked. I dread to think what would have happened if Martha and Brigitte hadn't pulled her off.'

'I'm fine, thanks,' she croaked, determined not to be moved by his concern. 'I'd rather stay here with Mum.'

* * *

Guy felt torn. He wanted to speak to Barbara Price and find out what happened to Greta, but he didn't want to leave Cara in the state she was in.

When he had arrived at the Potter house, having been phoned by Brigitte, he'd wanted to take Cara in his arms, only to find she had closed herself off to him.

That was apart from Martha Potter practically forming a barricade around her daughter. It was natural that a mother should be so protective, especially after what happened. It just made it difficult for Guy to get close to Cara and let her know how worried he was for her.

It pained him to hear how badly she sounded, but she seemed to be making it clear that she did not want his help or his concern.

'We'll call around in the morning,' was all he could say when Martha had forbidden any further contact with Cara for that day. He knew it made sense for her to rest her voice, but he was overwhelmed with frustration that he could not get her alone and find a way to make things right with her.

Haxby had magically produced a car from somewhere, and insisted that Guy and Brigitte let him take them to see Barbara Price, because he wanted to be there to see if she confessed. She had been moved from the police station to a hospital, in order to have her wounds from the car accident treated.

Guy was surprised when Haxby pulled into the grounds of a mental hospital. They were led along a maze of corridors, starting with bright, clean rooms and ending in dank hallways with metal doors. Misery oozed out of every wall.

'She's in high security,' Haxby explained. 'They tell me she's in a pretty bad way, so there will have to be a guard nearby at all times.'

Barbara Price sat in the corner of the bed, handcuffed to the metal headboard. Her normally neat and coiffured hair was all messed up and she had tear stains around her eyes. She started when she saw Brigitte.

'Greta, my love, you've come to me at last.'

Whatever sanity Barbara Price had clung on to seemed to have completely dissipated.

'I have,' said Brigitte, taking her hand and sitting next to her 'And I need to know, Lotte. How did you kill me?'

Guy had never been more proud of his niece at that moment. She was stronger than he was.

'Don't you remember, my love?'

'It's very difficult to remember things . . . on this side,' said Brigitte, glancing awkwardly at her uncle and Haxby.

'That witch brought you back, didn't she? The dirty little gypsy girl. She's been there all along, tormenting me, knowing about me. You didn't know, did you my love? I hid it from you.'

'Didn't know what?' Brigitte's eyes had flashed when Price insulted Cara, but she somehow managed to maintain her composure.

'That I'm not like others. That I don't feel emotion as others do. Except what I feel for you. That was real, my love, even when I killed you.'

'Why did you kill me, Lotte?'

'I had worked so hard with that idiot Eric Black. He was nothing when I found him. Just a nasty little burglar. But I saw potential there, as long as he did whatever I said. But you found me and I knew that all I had worked for would be wasted.'

'So you killed me? Was it the same way you killed the man and woman at the pub?'

'No, never.' Price shook her head vehemently. 'I would never have done that to you. I only meant to burn you after you died, when it couldn't hurt you anymore. I used Eric's insulin. So that even if you were found, no-one would guess. They'd just think that you staggered into the fire after suffering a heart attack. I had to stab the Anderson man. She nearly caught me then too. The gypsy girl.'

'And you burned down the pub with . . . ' Brigitte turned to Guy and raised a questioning eyebrow.

'Nancy and Sammy,' he said.

'You burned Nancy and Sammy?'

'I'm sorry about Nancy, but Sammy had to die. He was there on the night I buried you and he'd probably told her. I almost killed him and buried him alongside you, but he managed to knock me down and run away. He wasn't as stupid as I thought. Then he came back. Did he think I had forgotten?'

'What do you know about my . . . about Brigitte's father?' asked Brigitte.

'Schwartz!' Price almost spat the name out. 'You know all this, Greta.'

'I forget things here . . . on the other side . . . '

'It was only so you could get out of Germany. I had to know you were safe, my love. He'd been sniffing around you for years, so I told you to let him have what he wants and he'd get you out. I didn't expect you to marry him, but he wouldn't settle for anything less. You betrayed me, and in the end you gave birth to his brat!'

'Is there anything else you want to know?' Brigitte looked at Guy and then Haxby. Her eyes were awash with tears. Both shook their heads.

'One last thing,' Brigitte said. 'Where did you bury me?'

'Don't you even remember that?'

'How could I? I was dead.' Brigitte's voice had become hard and bitter.

'Up at the old Roman ruins in Midchester.'

Brigitte got up and rushed out of the room. Haxby followed her, but Guy stayed where he was. He waited until they had gone then he advanced on Barbara.

'If you were a man,' he said, savagely,

'I would kill you for what you did to my sister, to Anderson, to Nancy and Sammy. And for what you did to Cara today.'

'The gypsy girl?' Price laughed, maniacally. 'Oh don't say she's cursed you too. In the Fatherland we knew what to do with people like that.' She made a cut throat motion with her hand.

Guy clenched his fists. He had to leave the room before he did something he regretted later. The door clanged shut behind him and he took a deep, cleansing breath.

Haxby and Brigitte were in deep conversation in the hallway.

'Mr Haxby says she might never stand trial,' said Brigitte.

'The psychiatrist says she's been holding things together for so long that now she's completely lost it,' Haxby explained. 'Ironically, only the deception and the thought she was working for some higher cause gave her the illusion of sanity. The psychiatrist did put it in more technical terms, but it all amounts to the same. She's completely insane. Seeing Brigitte and believing she was Greta tipped her over the edge.'

'So she won't be punished?'

Guy desperately wanted to hit something. He chose a nearby wall and nearly broke his fingers. He clutched them to him and his voice rose in anger.

'She murdered four people, Haxby. She nearly killed Cara today. How can she just walk away from that?'

'She won't be walking away, Sullivan. She'll be locked up here for a long time.'

'Yes, and one day they'll pronounce her fit to leave, and she'll just walk out of here, take up a new identity and start again somewhere else.'

'That won't happen. Even if she went to trial, she won't be hanged. They repealed the death penalty last year.'

'I don't know that I want her to be hanged,' said Guy.

But deep down he knew he was lying; he wanted her to suffer just as Greta had suffered, and if he could not kill her himself, then he was quite happy to let someone else do it for him.

'I just want her to be punished.'

'I think she's her own punishment, Uncle Hans,' said Brigitte, taking him by the arm. 'She has to live every day with the thought that she murdered the only person she ever loved.'

'How can you be so forgiving, Brigitte?'

'I have to be. I've let what I saw as Mama's abandonment sour my whole life. Now I know she didn't abandon me, that she was stolen away from me. In many ways it makes things easier, even if it hurts that she suffered so badly at the hands of that woman. I have to move on now, and so do you. Wasn't that the reason you came to look for her? So we could both start to live again? Now you have a chance of happiness with Cara.'

'I think I burned my bridges there.'

'Then you don't know women at all, Uncle Hans.'

He stroked his niece's cheek affectionately. 'When did you get to be so wise?'

'I got it from my favourite uncle,' she said with a smile.

'I'm your only uncle.'

'You'd still be my favourite. Come on, let's get out of here.' Brigitte shivered. 'I don't like this place.'

Things felt far from over to Guy, with Barbara Price in a mental hospital instead of prison and Cara seemingly a million miles out of his reach.

As he walked out into wintery sunshine, he had a strange feeling of emptiness. For so long he had wanted to find out what happened to Greta. He had spent night after night imagining the worst. Now he knew the truth, there was a yawning chasm where the question had been.

When he was with Cara in the hotel room, making love to her, he had forgotten about Greta for a while. He had forgotten everything except the lovely young woman in his arms. After the shock of receiving the telegram, he had rushed her away, knowing from the look in her eyes that she was confused and upset. He had been sure she would understand when she knew the truth. But he had not even given her a chance to understand. Instead he had hurt her deeply.

And now he had lost her. That was the real emptiness inside him. In a short time, Cara had filled up his whole life and now all that was left was an aching void.

* * *

It was getting dark when the police set up a cordon around the Roman site. They had also put arc lights around the area. Guy stood just outside the cordon, wanting to join them. The police had made it clear that he would only be in the way.

After about half an hour, he felt movement at his side.

'Cara? What are you doing here? You

should be resting.'

'I heard the police were digging up here and came to see if I could be of any help,' she said, her voice still very strained. 'I mean, I thought Brigitte might need some female company. I'm sorry. If I'm in the way . . . '

'No, not at all. Actually I'm glad you're here, though it might not be pretty. Brigitte is over there, talking to Haxby.' He gestured to his niece. 'I think they're at the beginning of a beautiful relationship.'

'Yes, he does seem to like her very much. I think he's a nice man too.'

It pained Guy to hear Cara's voice. Every word was forced out. 'I still think you should rest your voice.'

'OK, I'll shut up then.'

He smiled. 'I didn't mean it like that. Thank you for coming up here.'

'I suppose I wanted to know how things ended.'

Guy explained what had happened with Barbara Price. 'They say she'll never stand trial.'

'Perhaps that's for the best,' Cara suggested. 'It will only prolong the agony for you and Brigitte.'

'Yes, I hadn't thought of it that way. It just doesn't feel like it's over, you know?'

'I'm sure it will take a while, after all the time you've waited.'

There was a shout from one of the policemen digging, followed by a flurry of movement. They had found her!

Guy only saw snatches of the body as they drew it out of the grave. He saw tattered rags and old newspapers and a mess of muddy blonde hair. But there was very little to identify the body as Greta. Still, he knew it was her. It couldn't be anyone else.

That was when his reserve failed him, he started to crumble, and tears fell down his cheeks.

Suddenly he felt himself embraced in tender arms.

'Shh, darling,' Cara murmured, stroking his hair, her tears mingling with his. 'It's all over now.'

15

The villagers had begun to wonder if the bonfire night celebrations would ever take place, so much had happened to disrupt the plans. Out of deference to Guy and Brigitte, they had even offered to cancel everything, including the Guy Fawkes competition. Guy, while appreciating the offer, insisted the celebrations proceed. He said it was not fair to cancel it because of the children who had been looking forward to it.

The fog that had been clouding the village since mid-October had finally cleared and it seemed as if they were going to be rewarded with a clear night sky.

The village hall was packed.

'If the pub was open, it wouldn't be so crowded,' Meredith Cunningham said wryly.

It was a subdued affair. It seemed as

if no-one really wanted to be seen to be enjoying themselves when there had been so much unhappiness in the past few weeks.

The children were thankfully oblivious to it all. Women had set up cake stalls, tombolas and raffles, and potatoes were baking in the oven in the kitchen. The aroma of sausages and onions filled the air as Mrs Simpson fried them and put them into buns for the children. Several times she swatted her hungry husband away, saying, 'Children first, Len!'

Cara sat with Peg Bradbourne and her mother, sipping lemonade. Eric Black stood a little away from everyone, looking completely lost.

'Come and join us, Eric,' said Peg, kindly.

'If I'm not intruding,' he said. Gone was the bravado that had always characterised him. He had thrown away all pretence, even having his hair cut and his sideburns shaved. Instead of his usual inappropriate fashions, he wore a sensible dark suit, over a V-neck sweater and white shirt.

'No, of course not,' said Cara. Rather than turn against him, the villagers mostly felt sorry for him. They could hardly do otherwise, considering Barbara Price had fooled everyone.

'Can I ask you something, Mr Black?' Cara ventured.

'Eric, please. Yes, go on. It can't be any worse than the questions the media have been asking me. I suppose I should understand, running a newspaper.' He laughed humourlessly.

'When we came to dinner, you seemed uncomfortable when Guy talked about the report in the newspaper. The one about the woman spy. Did you suspect Barbara then?'

'Yes and no. What can I say, Cara? I more or less lived with the woman for twenty years and I trusted her with everything. But when she said if I'd been away she would have hired an outside editor, she lied. She was in charge in my absence.'

He took a sip of his tea. 'The thing is, running a small town newspaper, you don't always have to be rigid about your sources. People believe anything if it's written down. You've probably all realised that much of what was written about my exploits in the Home Guard was made up. Barbara said it was to improve my image, because I hadn't fought in the war. I had to be seen to be brave, even if I wasn't.'

He sighed and went on, 'But it meant that we could publish just about anything, and as long as we didn't libel people or give too many details, we could make up stories. I think Barbara made up the story about the spy just in case people had seen Greta Mueller around town. Or maybe just in case young Sammy said anything. All she had to do was point to the story in the newspaper, and no-one would question it.'

'What will you do now?' asked Martha Potter.

'Standing for office is out of the

question now that it's known I have a criminal record, but I've still got the newspaper and my other business interests. They're legitimate by the way. I really did want to change my life, and Barbara told me she could help me do it. I sometimes felt like a marionette with her pulling the strings, but as I didn't have a clue how to reach out to people, I let her do it. And now she's escaped we'll probably never see her again anyway.'

'And now she's run away,' Peg Bradbourne repeated. They'd had word that morning that Barbara Price had somehow managed to get out of the sanatorium. Her whereabouts were unknown. 'It's probably for the best. I can't help feeling a little bit sorry for her.'

'Peg!' Cara exclaimed. 'She killed people . . . she killed Nancy. I'm sorry, Eric,' she added, turning to Black. His face was a mask of pain.

'You're right, Cara,' he said. 'I know she did terrible things.'

'Oh, I know she's a murderer, sweetheart,' Peg said. 'I'm not saying what she did was right. But from what I've heard she was desperately in love with Greta Mueller. We live in unforgiving times, even though everyone is supposed to be more open about sex nowadays. They are, but only about what they see as 'normal' sex. Anyone who doesn't fit into the neat little boxes that society builds for them is ostracised and, in the case of men, prosecuted.'

In full flow, Peg continued, 'Do you know that the only reason lesbianism isn't against the law is because Queen Victoria did not understand how it could happen and no-one wanted to explain it to her? I don't think we can begin to imagine what it must feel like to have to hide one's feelings.'

'It doesn't excuse murder,' said Cara. She lowered her voice in case anyone else was listening. 'After all, Mrs Abercrombie and Miss Watson are rumoured to be lesbians, but they don't go around murdering people.'

She would not feel sorry for Barbara Price, no matter what Peg said. Barbara — or Lotte — had killed Guy's sister and taken the lives of three more innocent people, and all to hide the fact that she was really a Nazi spy.

'Point taken,' said Peg.

'I'd better get going,' said Eric Black.

'Oh, I'm so sorry, Eric,' said Cara. 'I know this is hard for you, and I am sorry for you, really I am.'

'It's something I'll have to get used to, Cara. People will be talking about this for a long time to come. I'd rather they did it to my face than behind my back.'

He gave a tight smile and left them then a few seconds later, he left the village hall.

'Do you think he'll be alright?' Cara asked.

'It'll take time, but he'll survive,' said Martha. 'He's a fighter, that one.'

The Guy Fawkes competition was just about to begin when Guy Sullivan entered the village hall.

'I was asked to judge,' he explained to Cara and Meredith, who had the children lined up.

'Are you sure you want to?' asked Cara. 'After everything that's happened?'

'Like I said when you offered to cancel the party, I don't want the children to miss out.'

The atmosphere became lighter, mainly because Guy made such a point of enjoying himself looking at all the different Guy Fawke figures that the children had made. There was laughter when heads and arms fell off various Guys and mothers and fathers realised for the first time that their best clothes had been utilised.

'It's a good job we're not having a bonfire,' said one mother, rescuing her Sunday dress from one of the effigies.

'Oh come on,' said Guy, 'You've got to have a bonfire on bonfire night.'

'But we thought . . . ' Cara started to say.

'Never mind that. It's for the

children, remember?'

He awarded a prize — a voucher to buy sweets from Mr Fletcher's shop — to one of the children, and then insisted on organising the building of a bonfire up on the village green.

People brought out old chairs and other furnishings, along with tons of newspapers and other junk that they'd been longing to get rid of.

Cara could not imagine what it must have cost Guy to put aside his own pain in order to make sure that everyone in Midchester had a good time.

As the bonfire took hold and flames filled the night sky, she was suddenly aware of his arm around her shoulder.

'Thank you for this,' she said. 'It must be hard for you.'

'There's been too much unhappiness over the past few weeks,' he said. 'This should break the spell. Hopefully next year you won't all be thinking of Greta, Nancy and Sammy when you hold your bonfire night celebrations.'

'I don't think I'll be able to manage

that,' she said. Her eyes stung, but she didn't know if it was tears or the smoke from the bonfire. *And I won't be able to forget you either*, she thought.

'Where's Brigitte?' she asked, hoping to hide her emotions.

'She's packing to leave. And when Brigitte packs it's a military operation. We're going back to America this week and we're flying Greta's body back to be buried there. I've nothing against Midchester, but I think my mother will want to be able to visit her grave.'

'Of course.' Cara's heart plummeted in her chest like a stone. She always knew he would leave, but the thought of it was killing her. 'She must be devastated.'

'I think she always knew that Greta was dead, but I still want to see her, so she knows she still has family.'

'She'll be glad to see you both, I'm sure.'

'Cara, I'm sorry about the way I behaved at the hotel. And for the awful things I said to you last week.'

'Forget it,' Cara said, trying to sound casual. 'You had a lot on your mind, and I was being selfish.'

'No, you weren't. You're never selfish. You're the kindest person I know.'

'I'm glad that you've finally found out the truth,' she said, biting back tears. 'Even if that truth was terrible. You'll be able to move on now.' If nothing else, she and Guy could part as friends. Even if it was breaking her heart.

'Strange,' he said, looking down at her. His handsome face was illuminated by the light from the bonfire. 'I don't particularly want to move on.'

'I suppose you've lived with this for so long that it's hard to realise it's all over.'

'I'm not talking about Greta,' he said. 'I'm talking about you. Cara, I could have kicked myself when I was so unkind to you the other day. You didn't deserve it. Then when I heard that Barbara Price had nearly strangled you . . . '

He put his arms around her and pulled her in close.

'I wanted to kill her on that score alone. I've wanted to tell you so many times how I feel about you, but I kept putting it off because I was afraid my feelings for you would get in the way of finding Greta. I didn't want to forget about her again.'

'Of course not. I understand Guy. It was selfish of me to — '

He stopped her with a kiss that took her breath away.

'And I told you you're not selfish,' he said, when he finally pulled away from her. 'You're wonderful and beautiful and kind. I love you, Cara, and I want you to come to America with me. We can be married before we go. We'll get a special licence. I don't want to leave Midchester without you.'

'Marry you?' Though Cara's throat had healed, she suddenly found herself unable to speak again.

'Yes, if you'll have me.'

'Of course I'll have you!' she cried,

throwing her arms around his neck. 'I was so afraid I'd never see you again, and I love you, Guy! I love you so much.'

As they kissed again, a volley of fireworks exploded, lighting up the night sky.

Cara pulled away, smiling ecstatically. Before she could say another word, there was a shout of alarm from the crowd. She turned and saw someone hurtling towards her.

For a horrible moment, Cara thought that one of the effigies on the bonfire had come to life. The creature coming towards her had dishevelled hair and waved her arms wildly like some grotesque scarecrow.

'You!' The creature screamed holding what looked like a knife. 'You little witch!'

Cara had no real thoughts of harming Barbara Price, she simply responded to the attack by holding up her hands and pushing the madwoman away from her.

Barbara Price staggered, her arms windmilling as she struggled to maintain her balance, but she failed and as she fell back into the bonfire she was rapidly engulfed in flames.

All anyone could do at first was watch in horror.

What seemed like ages later, but was in fact only a few seconds, several men rushed forward trying to pull her out, but the flames were too strong.

Suddenly someone grabbed her feet and pulled her out of the inferno that way.

Herbie Potter took off his coat to try and douse the flames surrounding Price's body, but it was too late.

Barbara Price was dead.

Guy held Cara in his arms as she sobbed.

'Shh, darling,' he whispered. 'Now it really is over.'

We do hope that you have enjoyed reading this large print book.

Did you know that all of our titles are available for purchase?

We publish a wide range of high quality large print books including:
Romances, Mysteries, Classics
General Fiction
Non Fiction and Westerns

Special interest titles available in large print are:
The Little Oxford Dictionary
Music Book, Song Book
Hymn Book, Service Book

Also available from us courtesy of Oxford University Press:
Young Readers' Dictionary
(large print edition)
Young Readers' Thesaurus
(large print edition)

For further information or a free brochure, please contact us at:
Ulverscroft Large Print Books Ltd.,
The Green, Bradgate Road, Anstey,
Leicester, LE7 7FU, England.
Tel: (00 44) **0116 236 4325**
Fax: (00 44) **0116 234 0205**

Other titles in the Linford Romance Library:

SEEK NEW HORIZONS

Teresa Ashby

Sister Dominique, already having serious doubts about her calling, is sent on a mercy mission to South America after a devastating earth-quake. There, she meets Dr Steve Daniels, and feelings she had never expected to experience again are stirred up. As she is thrown into caring for a relentless stream of casualties, her thoughts are in turmoil. How will she cope in the outside world if she leaves the sisterhood? And dare she allow herself to fall in love again?

HOUSE OF FEAR

Phyllis Mallett

Jill's twenty-first birthday is more than just a milestone — it marks the day her life changes forever . . . A letter arrives on the morning of her birthday; an invitation to travel to Crag House on the remote Scottish island of Inver to stay with the grandfather whose existence she had been completely unaware of. Whilst there, she meets her cousins, Owen and George, and handsome neighbour Robert Cameron. But her visit has involved her in a web of deceit that may threaten her life . . .

SUSPICIOUS HEART

Susan Udy

When Erin discovers that her mother's home and livelihood is under threat from the disturbingly handsome Sebastian, she knows she has to fight his plans every step of the way. However, she quickly realises Sebastian is equally determined to win, and he apparently has the backing of the entire village. When a campaign of intimidation is begun against Erin and her mother, it doesn't take her long to work out that it can only be Sebastian behind it . . .

THE RUNAWAYS

Patricia Robins

When Judith and Rocky elope to Gretna Green they sincerely believe marriage will solve all their problems. But the elopement proves to be the beginning of an entirely new set of difficulties . . . Rocky begins to wonder if his parents were right — is he even in love? Were they too young after all? And in the background Gavin, Judith's boss, watches her disillusionment with a concern which is growing into something more . . .

ANGEL'S TEARS

Teresa Ashby

Born in the same year that the Titanic sank, seventeen-year-old Cassandra Grant has the world at her feet. But tragedy strikes her family and Cassie has to grow up fast. She falls in love with Dr Michael Ryan — but then discovers he is about to be engaged to be married. Cassie leaves town to begin training as a midwife and tries to forget Michael, but tragedy strikes again and she has to return home where there are more surprises in store . . .

DEADLY INHERITANCE

Phyllis Mallett

1927: Sarah Morton is looking forward to starting her new job as a tutor with a wealthy Yorkshire family, but she is taken aback when her young charge, Justin Howard, claims that someone wants him dead — and his great-grandfather seems to believe the same. Could greed be a motivating factor in the attempts to see off the young heir? And is Justin's handsome Uncle Adam really to be trusted?

OKANAGAN REGIONAL LIBRARY
3 3132 03520 5162